Dear Reader:

I've been a big fan and a friend of Jessica Holter for many years and I'm happy to be able to collaborate with her on this project. I hope that people will enjoy it.

Many of you may be familiar with the Punany Poets by their performances and appearance on HBO's *Real Sex*.

Erotic poetry has exploded over the past decade with passion being the key element. Jessica Holter, the self-professed "love child," has taken it to another level in this work. I've seen the future of the new sexual revolution and it's the Punany Poets' *Verbal Penetration*.

Zane

Jessica Holter's *The Punany Poets*

Verbal
Penetration

Strebor Books

New York London Toronto Sydney

Strebor Books
P.O. Box 6505
Largo, MD 20792
http://www.streborbooks.com

ISBN 13: 978-1-59309-112-5
ISBN 10: 1-59309-112-5
LCCN 2006938901

Cover design: Jessica Holter
Photo by Femi Andrades

First Strebor Books hardcover edition April 2007

10   9   8   7   6   5   4   3   2   1

Manufactured in the United States of America

For information regarding special discounts for bulk purchases,
please contact Simon & Schuster Special Sales at 1-800-456-6798
or business@simonandschuster.com

Dedication

To patience.
To The Womb that makes all life possible.

Special Thanks & Acknowledgments

To Jane Therese Brenner

To the Punany Family and the Punany Fans. To Zane & The Strebor family. To Paul Levine & Suzanne de Passe

To Keaton my reason.

To Sven Hamilton, Yulonda Washington & Angel II. To Terenda. To HBO's *Real Sex* producers, Katie Smallhere and Patti Kaplan.

To DJ Blackmon, Branden & Mrs Pernell, Keno Mapp, Femi, jus' BEA, Mohogany, Eebony, Ernest, Traci Bartlow, Dayna Gaspard, Gary McCoy & Nafissa, AMAN, Dwayne "Patrice" Wiggins. To Tisa, Shauna B., Kween, Shiela, Sonnie & London & and all the dancers & singers who bring the text to life... Punany's Pearl, Slam Most of All to my constant friend and Lover, to "Punany" - The vision.

Table of Contents

Verbal Penetration

BY *Ghetto Girl Blue*

Let us pray.

Let us ask
the Mother Goddess
to guide our fingers as they caress
our hearts,
as we open
our bodies,
as they receive one another.

Let us ask the God's for trust, worthiness of it
and understanding one to another.

And where there is danger,
let us look together into the night
that hosts our ancestors
begging them for guidance away from it.

Let us wash our bodies.

Let us stand naked in the light
before one another and praise
nature's most divine art.

Let there be no fear between us.

Let there be good loving
that is as warm and as safe as
the womb which is our center.

Let our bodies be great vessels
feeding positive energy into the world
as we fuck.
Let us talk about sex.
Let us fuck while we do it.
Let us strap on the armor
suited for modern times,
squeeze ourselves into
the thin line
between lust and love
and jack them off.

Just to keep it hot,
we will extend an open invitation to
prostitution
porn
and
molestation.

Let us be on one accord as we
enter through the gates of the
Sexual Revolution
so that our enemies will find only
solidarity amongst our ranks.
We will ask Poetry to have that
smooth brother, "Music"
To pace this erotic escapade ...
with bass deep enough
to skinny dip in.

Let us lick.
Let us bite.
Let us
cuss and cum together

Let us
let our hair down
and sweat.

We will laugh like children
as we play with our toys.

Let us mentally masturbate.

Let us mentally masturbate.

May we know no fear
as we take this erotic journey
through the darkest valleys
and highest peaks of

Verbal Penetration.

...and

Just when you thought
it was safe
to stop coming...

Let us begin again.

Let us fuck.

Hey

BY *Jessica Holter*

"Hey,"
he said
a cheek full of chew
picking up the pink bouquet
talking to the minister but
addressing him as "your honor,"

Tell me again
why a dead whore
needs flowers in hell.

Pushing the flowers
into his wife's arms,
he spat chew into his
once lover's grave.

Punany Narration

BY *Ghetto Girl Blue*

My foster mother said I talk too much.
My pastor said I had the gift of gab.
Everybody thought I was fast.
AIDS came out of nowhere, just when I had become an
entertainment journalist, writing chronicles of backstage antics.
Before anyone knew what hit them, Punany was born;
Born of my memories of rape and molestation; Born of the
similar stories women told me; Born of the shock of Eazy E's
untimely death. See sex was raised by an uninhibited,
dictating father who could only love a bound pussy, and a
mother with one foot shackled to the stove and the other
to a bed post.

Punany is the culmination of erotic words, laced through
soulful grooves, laid on top of a funk-stained hip-hop dance
bed. She is bold. She is powerful. She knows just who she is
and whose mind she wants to fuck into the wee hours of the
Sexual Revolution.

The PUNANY POETS were some sassy writers, with more
guts than any G I ever knew. We didn't have money, or many
friends. Most of the third eye poetry community had its
revolutionary tongue stuck like a needle on a scratched 45...

The revolution will not be televised.
The revolution will not be televised.
The revolution will not be televised.
Punany busted on the television screen like,
Badddamn!
The revolution is between my thighs,
let the fearful beware
Her soldiers do not apologize.

Casting Satan

BY *Jessica Holter*

Before you
command
Satan to
get thee
behind you...
make sure
that
God
has
your
back.
Otherwise
keep that
demon
where
you can see him.

Your Black Fist

BY *Ghetto Girl Blue*

I want my mouth
to speak nothing but praise
when speaking of you
My beautiful black messiah

I want to be the key
to the rusty cage
that imprisons black love
use me

I want to love you
as I love my own hands
with necessity
with appreciation
with respect

In the bedroom
In the boardroom
In the street
and at the table
give you respectable
representation

expecting only truth
of you
never fearing it

I want to be a queen who
makes you proud too
One who makes you understand
that making love to me is
among your most noble deeds
In me your seed is not wasted
but savored and manifested
before it is measured & devoured
broken down and regenerated
on my tongue and through my womb
in the game of your school
as historic files of your pedigree

I want to work out the kinks
of my trying childhood socialization
and inferior education with you
share fantasies and dreams
make plans to follow through
Verbally arrest you
before working the kinks
back into our hair
Lay and cool down in our sweat

I want to be your stairs
where there were only flat lands
to let down my hair for you
to climb into heaven

I want to be the chant
in your railroad song
and to go the distance
of the track with you

Like the Panthers
insist
like Montgomery bus strikers
persist
in the taking of our destiny
into our own hands

I want to be the revolution
in your black fist

I want to be the revolution
in your black fist

Thick

BY *Ghetto Girl Blue*

labels do not define me
I am rich with this
It matters not what I wear

Swelling with promise
Uncompromising
and as strong
as the thighs that guide my independence

I am a diva
Cloaked
with possibility
Empowered
by my freedom
to take pride in every
part of me

I am a warrior
My heart
is my shield and sword

I am the light
Breaking through
the seams of night

I am the lioness
dogs find in the moon
the stars
highlight the coils
of my mane

I am a Goddess
My skin has been kissed
by the Son

I am the Mother of Nurture
The world is cradled
in my hips

I am thick with this

Make Love in Love, and **be safe** always. Gone are the days when AIDS was a disease reserved for gays.

AIDS is a **pandemic,** with no respect of person, lifestyle, or religious preference... It kills **indiscriminately,** destroying not only lives, but generations through the heterosexual female womb.

In 1995 **heterosexual sex** accounted for **10 percent** of all AIDS cases; today it accounts for **90 percent** of all new infections.

— **National Centers for Disease Control and Prevention**

Let me Tell you about My Pimp

BY *Ghetto Girl Blue*

Let Me Tell You About my Pimp

My pimp is hard as nails
he never fails
to give me what I ask for
but to be sure...
I want only what he wants for me.
My pimp brought a million souls to foreign shores
and bound us all to twisted morals
There is no loyalty like a whore's
When faced with freedom
she lightly coos
Sweet daddy please don't leave me

Why I Love You

BY *Jessica Holter*

Why I love you
you ask and I open my mouth
to obediently tell
as if shouting from a high mountain

Because you believed
in me
when I didn't believe in myself
Because you always want more
and better
and you make me better
and to strive
for more every day

Because your love for me
is so real
is so strong
is so deep
even you do not understand it

the poet
can not explain it

so rich is this love
only God can own it

I love you, my love
because your love and my love
are the same love
Because you love the people
the things
the life all around you
with a realness I have never known
until knowing you

Because I love to Lay
with you even when we are only
sleeping

I toss in my slumber
for fear of missing your heart beat

I love you, my love
Because we share the dream
even when
the dream changes course

Lady of Poetry

BY *Jessica Holter*

Shssh huh, Shssh huh
Shssh huh, Shssh huh
Shssh huh, Shssh huh

I was tending to
minding my business
the other day,
exercising a little For'Play
on the proverbial
nakedness of poetry
when somebody choked the future
out of her democracy

That lady of poetry

Somebody said the revolution would not be televised
But I got a cancellation notice on my two-way last night.

As she lay
Spread before me,
Beckoning
this writer's
tongue to lap

at her walls
and drink
from her well of words,
I became immersed in the verse of her
Body's song

Her heartbeat embraced the rhythm of
my breath
and we made music
all our own

Shssh huh, Shssh huh
Shssh huh, Shssh huh

And in the crescendo
of our melody
her prophecy
came to me like an epiphany

Her eyes cried the psalm of late poets
whose verses were heard only
after the Earth's consumption
of their flesh

They said her soldiers were guilty of treason
for leaving her on a battlefield far away,
to die in the enemy territory of SLAM, USA

Her stretch marks mapped time traveled
by bloodied feet of slaves,
her vagina exuded a tartness
that hinted of crack babies' graves,
That lady of poetry, she made love to me

Shssh huh, Shssh huh

Until we were ugly
and we were pretty
and we were everything
and we were nothing

and we were only just beginning
and we were Omega
as we were dance —

and we were soft
and we were gritty
and we were not
one Punany
but many, many, many
pieces of love and pieces of grief
falling on to tear-stained pages of
time's resistance

That Lady of Poetry!

Her breasts were swollen with the
hope of her dark past
her hips curved gently
into the full promise
of her strong thighs
I tucked her hand into the shadow of my red locks,
turned my mouth to kiss her palm,
She traced my lips with a writer's crimped fingers
and dug deeper inside me,
than any man ever could have

Somebody said the Revolution would not be televised
but I got a cancellation notice on my two-way last night.

They said, in spite of all of our sex education,
AIDS is still on the rise
and in spite of our determination,
we are still self-victimized

They said, in spite of our cooperation,
we gorge ourselves with
political rhetoric
thinking ourselves young politicians
and become as the pig we claim not to eat
wallowing in the spoils of gentrification
no place to lay our heads

for we dread any place intrusive enough to call itself "Home"

So we roam
through knowledge, unknown
forging forward on an escaped goat
with empty pens as swords

They told me
Nonviolence took one in the face for the race
to ambivalence
where the dollar defines our opinions
The Black Panther Party for Self Defense
was sedated heavily
Somebody said they found the
Black Panthress dead, three blows to the head,
Sprawled on a bed with post mortem levity
Yeah, if you ain't heard,
somebody said the Revolution
was on her way when she was overtaken
by a team of power thieves
Apathy, "The Hater"
Civil Rights, "The Liar"
Inertia, "The Indolent"
Cowardice, "The Menace"
and on the authority of "Welfarism"
her soldiers were hoarded to concentration
encampments called "Projects"
packed in square blocks between freeways,
scientifically financial experiments

But everybody was just trying to forget,
getting Hiiiiiigh!
as ideals became dealing, guts became guns
children begat checks, got taxpayers upset,
private industry flexed,
prison became an industrial complex,
privatized timeshares for industry to clock in
even Victoria's Secret got stock in
The Lady, I'm told, donned her rags to the track

Yeah, that Lady of Poetry
took to the stroll to make herself whole

Because the Revolution was cancelled
due to Niggativity

But I,
never told a soul,
just opened up my door
and let that gangster whore
climb right on inside of me

Shssh ahhh.

Revolution of a Poet

BY *Ghetto Girl Blue*

Say sista?

How much is it gon' cost you
To lend me your ear?

Brotha man?
What's the price for me to share
A slice of my life
Over this mic?

And just how many revolutions I got to start
To keep the applause coming?

How long are you going to keep the padlock
On my panties before you will grant me
The right to heal myself
Like Tupac, chill myself
With vicarious life of poetic psalm

Like Sonia, I write
Like Sonia, I do so
So I don't have to kill anyone

When I heard her words
Resounding through my mind

With the force of my own voice
I was shocked to hear them
I laughed just a little bit, to hear them
and was soothed to feel them
Wrap themselves around
My kind of fear of death

I ain't "Martin," been to the mountain top
Ain't fearing any man, "Luther"
seen the promised land, "King"
I ain't ashamed to say
I fear death
But then, I ain't subscribing
To a school of thought
That eases that sort of thing

I fear death; I do
Much the same way as
I feared the tippy pausin'
Eel skin squeak
Of my daddy's shoes
As he crept into my room
Lay atop of me
Spewing
Contradiiiiiiiicktions
To the Christian stewardship
Rhetoric that first hipped me to the difference
Between talkers and doers
fighters and dreamers
and all the
Beaten Ghetto Cinderellas
and drinking Dead Janes
and every female reading these lines
loving daddies who are incapable of knowing the difference
between
loving a girl child and abusing her
loving a woman and fucking her

creating shame and fits of rage,
his deaf ear fell on my
screaming kicking soul as he dragged my limp body
to a place where sun, moon and stars are never cast
distorted lies, his threatening eyes
my tender thighs spread wiiiiide

sex and death they dawn the same mask in this place that
harbors my fear
thief in my temple of innocence
using this, abusing this, confusing this
til only the devil remembered my name
then he adds blame to my shame
forsaking womanhood with ooooh got damn baby girl
God Damn you for looking so good
The only daddy I've every known,
killed me a little more each time
his sweet deacon minty tongue slipped
into my speechless mouth
and you betta not neva tell nobody, don't tell nobody
nobody but who?
would listen to a Ghetto Girl Blue?
Caught in red tape raptures
whose only answer was another doctored,
fostered fake as getting paid "family"
I use the term loosely

The pad became my sister,
the pen my brother,
the paper my mother
The Punany Poets my ministry

and so I write

Freedom of words blew breath
Into me until I was revived
And now Punany saves my life
Keeping me alive, maybe save
someone else's life

Verbal Penetration

A little rhyme at a time
So to all the third eye
Motherfuckers
Hating on my kind of fear of death
Hating on Punany yet loving GGB
Still not understanding me
Don't even own a gun or even
Possess a permit
Talking about Revolution
Revolution
Revolution
That's pure rhetoric
Revolution that's pure rhetoric
Telling me
Don't you talk about Punany
Don't you talk about Punany
Don't talk about Punany!
Well fuck me!
For wanting to make
Love ...   Not war
And so I write, and so I write
Like Sonia Sanchez,
I write
So I don't have to, kill anyone

Pussy Willow

BY *Dwayne Wiggins* AND *Jessica Holter*

I wanna make love to a Scorpio,
Lay back with this Aquarius cuz here we go...

Ask out hearts to be fair with us
making love in public places cuz they're daring us
ghetto birds in the night trying to stare at us
this is the age of Aquarius again
and I'm still your best friend

Pussy willow,
Won't you let me touch you from head to toe
I don't wanna stop until we let go
Pussy Willow

Come and go with me, Papi flow with me
this feels like poetry, the way you're digging me
Picture this, my thighs spread cheek to cheek
and my ass on your pillow

Punany's the name but you can call me pussy willow

I wanna make love to a Scorpio,
Lay back with this Aquarius cuz here we go...

In the Beginning

BY *Ghetto Girl Blue*

In the beginning was the word
and the word was with God
and the word was God
and the word was filtered through the tongues of man
blaming the fall of himself on a woman.
Now he fears his weakness for her.
Now she fears her strength may drive him out of her garden.

Since 1995
From the ghetto, to the stage to the studio
from the open mic, to the printed page, to HBO
From CD to DVD to Video
Punany is the womb of spoken word.
You may not understand the power of Punany
but you need her for your very existence.
So at the world insistence
she let it flow
from ancient scroll, to the cross, to the grave
then ascending again
on the international stage
turning persecution into retribution
turning poetry into an institution

turning molestation into revolution
for a single cause
Life... and life more abundantly
All praise the first dame to dare
give it up one time for Eve!
...the original sinner serving fresh fruit for dinner!
She will eat of the fruit while they hide behind trees
She will embody the lamb while they spend wages to slam
and when she is lifted up
She will draw all men unto herself.
For you see... if you respected her
She would have no cause to be
so open
bra-burning
free
Call her what you want
but her name is "Punany"

Little Riddle

BY *Jessica Holter*

Three words for Punany
Your eyes are coasting my anatomy
Learning one life time, could not
reveal one half of me
My coyly knocking knees
Hips of a woman twice my age
Creamy skin with brown freckled maze
Pink satin tongue licks, thick lips as I speak
provoking phrases that raise
so much more than your questions
Three words for Punany?
Let's see,
I'm not in the bed;
I'm in your head
The little one Papi, up top
I could give me to you easy
or just sit back and let you watch me please me
'cause you know I'm kind of skeazy
A little cash can make a good girl sleazy
Don't want the dick if it's cheesy
If at any time this gets too greasy

pad your knees, and let cunnilingus bring us
to a most compelling
oooh stop!

You could slap it just a little
or just fiddle with this riddle
or ride straight down to the middle
until we both cop
Now close your eyes, daddy
and allow your mind to take you
to places soft and tender, warm and wet
as nice or as nasty as you want to get

Imagine, my mouth on your mouth
and my tongue... wherever you want it
Imagine pouring vanilla droplets of my love
into bottles and storing it up for rainy days
or savoring saccharine flavoring of my love's glaze
from each finger it plays
deep inside my depraved cave

Imagine, I'm licking the salt of your sweat
from your neck, down your back, through your crack, to your
black sack
I back into your shaft like a Mack truck
Then gulp your tequila secretions until I am drunk
And there is not one inch of your body, I have left to suck
Now pleasure pause and with a little luck
You'll get a clue
Three words for my Punany?

A Mind Fuck

Great Men Say

"God formed her body to belong to a man, to have and to rear children. Let them **bear children** till they die of it." — Martin Luther.

"In pain shall you bear children, your **urge** will be for your husband, and he shall rule over you."

— Genesis 3:16. Holy Bible

"Your women are fields to **cultivate**, so go to your fields as you will!"

— The Koran 2:223.

Transcend

BY *Ghetto Girl Blue*

Transcend sexual barriers with me
I am The Head Doctor.

In this house there are many rivers.

Sweet to the tongue,

Sour to the stomach,

Death to the heart,

Wet to the dick,

Electric to the clit,

Raw to the touch

Body parts and body smells
Many secrets to unveil
Many lies to un-tell

In her center there are
Deadly Heavens,
Brilliant Hells
Lynch trees that bend to
Blackened will

She is the darkness and the light
The wicked and the righteous
Fucking like dogs
In the mind's eye
She is PUNANY.

To all of the women who have been
Virgins turned whore and back again...
She is your best friend
This is her house,
and I am her servant here.

This is a safer sexual affair
Where ideas are served tartar,
Raw as the truth of naked feet on hot coals
So, if you're ready to take this erotic and soul testing journey,
take off your shoes, but
leave on your hat

The Male G-Spot

BY *Jessica Holter*

Yes Ladies, men have a G-Spot.
Though, scientifically known as the "prostate-perineum,"
Punany would just like to guide your attention to the dime-
sized soft spot between the anus (ass) and scrotum (his balls).
All of the nerves that control the erection, the orgasm, and
ejaculation
come together in the prostate and the perineum area.
So, if you are not stimulating this area, you are not taking him
to the heights his body is prepared to go and you wonder to
yourself
"Why oh why, are the men on the down-low?"

So,
even if you have a man who is a bit anal retentive,
promise him that you won't yell it if he don't tell it
Qualify your offer if you must,
offer him an in-office blow job every hump day of the month if
he does not cum... when you:

1. Gently engage in extended foreplay and fellatio.
2. Apply a finger condom to your index finger.
3. Let your tongue work its way to his prostate.
4. Lubricate this ass hole generously.
5. Massage it on the outside until the tension starts to give.
6. Insert only part of your finger into his ass.
7. Gently work it around, massaging
8. Slowly begin to move your finger in and out
9. Then let your finger call "Come here! Come here, dear boy!"
Curling it upwards...
Rubbing. Tapping. On his prostate
10. all the while your mouth and hand team up in a
pumping and sucking orgy of motion and sound

and pop!
swallowing is not recommended
he probably wouldn't even notice if you did.

I promise, you won't even have to pay that hump day debt,
but just to keep it hot, do it anyway...

You probably wonder now if this means he's gay
or goes both ways
who is to say? Like the power of Punany,
there lives
the power of the prostate.

The Head Doctor

BY *The Head Doctor*

I won't lie, I don't lie. I give good head.

And my truth is naked, but protected
Like the sensual elixir
that fills your love glove

When I exercise my skills,
Blessing you with seductive thrills
as the pink rose petal lips of my
café au lait with extra cream skin
whisper wetness and
repeat rhythms, repeat rhythms
to your monumental extension

My hands also know their craft.
They play your skin flute
with the careful expert skill,
a finely tuned instrument deserves.

And this Doctor's tongue,
Like a satin-coated homing device, she
probes beyond your proud outward gesture
to that hidden underneath place,

as my long eyelashes give butterfly kisses to your
Generation sack.

I won't lie, I don't lie, I could
Suck a golf ball through a yaaaaaaaaaaaaaaaaaaaaard
of garden hose
"What?" Do you ask, "Can Punany do for you?

Just mind fuck with me tonight
Mind Fuck
Mind who you fuck.

Giving Good Head

BY *DJ Blackmon*

Safety first, you know, it's true
So here's the first thing you should do
Middle and index finger together, condom on top
Insert in mouth, lightly suck, and once it opens then stop.
On the top of the head and over the crown,
Suck, then gently roll the edges down

Next there are many things you can do
To make you lover's dreams come true
Lips firmly round the head, up and down then lightly lick
All around the tip, butterfly flicks.

Fingers wrapped around the shaft,
Stroke it gently not too fast.
Lips lock firmly round
As your head bobs up and down
Slide it gently past your teeth and back
But softly, gently, must not scratch.

Let your tongue travel up and down licking the length
the entire trip,
Back to the crown lick all around and rub wet lips across the tip.
And as he slides in and out, your tongue gently caressing,
Stroke up and down until your lover gets his blessing.

X Visions of You

BY *Branden Pernell*

Stand up,in your high pumps
Buck naked, so I can see your firm legs
and your chocolate rump
Please strike a sexy pose
Like them Mary Joe's
from magazines and videos
"Or better yet...dance
...Like that
So I can see your kitty cat
Moving back and forth
Jiggle it baby, go head baby
Yeah that looks good
That's got me on
Like petrified wood
I wish I could get a taste
Of your secret place
Never would I rush it.

I'd always continue
In a slow...steady...pace
And check the expressions
On your face
As you writhe in ecstasy
Together you and me
Bodies moving in spasms
As we both bust Phat orgasms
The first...of...a couple
So supple is your skin
I wanna tell all my friends
How wonderful you are
My chocolate...star, and I
...your caramel bar
But don't bite me, baby
Just let me melt
In your mouth as you...
Oooh...! Let me stop
These visions are becoming
Too much for me,
Driving me crazy
So clear I can almost see
My visions of... thee
In the XXX variety

Lips Like Those

BY *DJ Blackmon*

Can you tell me what it's all about,
Walking around with your mouth poked out?

With lips like those, imagine
the wonder you could do
A smile like that and lips like those
what magic must come through

With lips like those,
the words you say hang, drip, or flow
but never pass unnoticed
as around your mouth they seem to play

I get mesmerized, just watching the way
You do what you do,
when you, say what you say

I watch them and imagine, how wonderful it might be
to feel their kiss or have them caressing any part of me
With lips like those,
you could stop a fighter in his tracks
and cause a healthy man to have
a sudden heart attack
(Dial 911, Dial 911)

With lips like those,
you could tell me to do almost anything
it's heaven just to watch you talk
a blessing to hear you sing

With lips like those, imagine
how well those lips could suck you
So soft and sensuous,
they make me want to fuck you

Can you tell me what it's all about,
Walking around with your mouth poked out?

With lips like those, I imagine
it isn't hard to please ... a pair of lips
that look like those,
with a pair of lips like these

Don't scream, don't shout, just pout
That's right, baby
Stick those luscious lips out.
Don't scream
Don't shout
Just pout.

Elixir

BY *J Steal*

It was like licking a wound
not bleeding but dying to be bled

I stabbed her again and again
with the sharpness of my tool
speaking to her in tongues
she translated the secrets of her Upper Room

I listened, anxiously heard and generously applied
all that I learned, Urgent...ly

Massaging my tightening jaw with her thighs
I faced womanhood without compromise
and ran the tempting trail of life with a gentle stride
Running the good race
fearing with respect
my partner and opponent

At first there came a piercing scream
then silence filled the halls of heaven
She flooded the killing fields
and stilled my tongue
with the Champagne of Venus
With her revolution came a great quake

an unstable ground upon which no man can stand
hiding her face from me
blushing so that I could not see her selfish conclusion
this illusion, yet, swelled my pride

(Besides, the elixir of her power and truth
had me a little warm and fuzzy inside.)
I was just a visitor in her Upper Room
A sinner by all counts
only flirting with salvation,
foolishly trusting a soap box preacher
not even aware of what manner of man
had confessed here before me

I rinsed my mouth and washed her down
Checked my breath against my palm
called my wife and went home.

I kissed her, as soon as I walked in the door.
Secretly wishing
she could taste the elixir
of untamed sex on my breath
but remaining silent in her suspicions,
she would simply be turned on
and somehow, she too, could become
as this Goddess of the Sun
wielding power without control
Oh! if my wife was the kind of woman,
a man could never own.

Call Before you Cum

BY *Kenita James*

Intimacy misses me
'Cause my man disses me
whenever I offer my love
But he's a good provider, a real father to his kids
Only, he works so hard that his eyelids
are the only things I can kiss
as he slips into deep sleep
I'm not a freak on a midnight creep
Not looking for a friend, a lover or even a dick
We could safely get hot and you won't get shot
If you jot your number on this napkin
and get in where you fit in
as my telephone trick

Don't laugh, brother, naw, don't bother
'cause this is quite an offer
Like Billy in case you didn't know it
Honey, I'm kind of a poet
Give me a chance to show it
and with my voice I'll blow it
My roll is on, don't try to slow it

'Cause I've got wet secrets I want to tell
The kind if lived could send me to hell
The kind when told on the telephone line
could slowly, and boldly seduce Ma Bell

We could talk about your absolute pleasure
Or my fantasy of you and me and her
Or the image of you gettin' it
As threatening skies open and we are both dripping wet
I'll bet you're wonderin' exactly how
to make my love come down
No one can do it better, or can get it any wetter
than I can with my own hand
I'll teach you well, until you understand
and you can work it like any woman
Push the button on the speaker phone
Whether you're at work or at home

Give me a call if you got the balls
and I'll get real specific
'cause my mind is quite prolific
but death is scientific
and honey,
 I don't do house calls

Pretty Black Babies

BY *J Steal*

Remember our first night together?

Your body just danced in my hands?
It was as magic as Motown
as healing as that unforgettable sound.

Slow and tempered
we taught rhythm the meaning of herself.

Sliding, skin on skin,
only our scent between us
washing in the old school R&B
that our folks made love to.

You were gentle with me
I was gentle with you also
I showed you ways to make love without
surrendering your virginity
and you were so grateful to me
You gave me your trust and your heart

I know it's only been
1 year, 6 months, 4 days, 3 hours, and 10 minutes
since we met...

Give or take a few.
But I do believe,
I want to spend the rest of my life with you,
making pretty Black babies,
to the same Funk Brothers music
that our folks made love to.

I have your trust and your heart
Now lady, please, give me your hand
Take this ring,
and make me
Your Husband.

Abstinently Yours

BY *D J Blackmon*

It took 2 long years of being devout
No drugs, No drinks, No men
I was completely going without
but feeling complete within.

When I was getting it regularly
I felt I was under attack
But it's been so long, I can say
I finally got my virginity back.

Then out of nowhere
Where nobody was suppose to be
came this Mack disguised as
Somebody who claimed to love me.

Whispering sweet "I don't know what's" in my ear
Saying the most fantastically sexual things I ever did hear
With safety on his tongue and sweetness on his lips
my body succumbed to the lure of the call of his finger tips.

Turned, twisted, probed, and penetrated
in every possible way
And once again, like before,
I had given my virginity away
and once he was done,
had had all his fun
He had nothing else to say.
After all that,
some say I deserve what I get,
for saving up my virginity
and giving it away for SHIT!!!

Passion and Mary Jane

BY *Branden Pernell*

My most memorable sexcapade was a situation that was fluke. I met this chic at the fruit stand of the Whole Foods Store. She was pickin' up strawberries and passion fruit. Since I had never experienced them before, I asked her to describe the passion fruit's taste. She looked me dead in my face, and with full, luscious lips said, "Passion."

So, as she was pickin' out a few good passions for me to try, my copy of "Punany Psalms" caught her eye. She was instantly intrigued by the title and wondered of its contents. When I told her of its erotic nature and safe sex themes she seductively smiled as if suddenly, sexually aroused... which led me to ask her name. And with those full, luscious lips she replied... "Mary Jane." We began to discuss the sensuality of the passion fruit and the aphrodisiac powers of strawberries. Our conversations led us to the checkout stand together; which led us to the parking lot, outside; which led us to our cars that were parked ironically, next to each other. She invited me to her home, which, she said, was nearby, to taste a piece of the passion and to continue our dialogue.

So I did.

We got to her pad, and Mary Jane said she had a bit of wine. I told her that was fine with me. So we continued to talk and drank a little Asti Spumante... and talked a little; and sipped a little; and as we sipped the convo went from sexy fruit to sexy people; from sexy music and dance to sexy clothes and lingerie; to sex and favorite sex positions and toys.

We discovered that we really had a lot in common.

All that talk of sex gave me quite a stiff bone and I could tell that she had a jones for me.

We lusted for and were diggin' one another when she decided to demonstrate her prowess in the art of fellatio. She pulled out a chocolate-flavored condom and proceeded to apply it with only her mouth. I let out an "Aye Mommie," cuz I was sprung on how she did what she did to me. I was able to bust in her mouth without her havin' to spit and she didn't have to worry about swallowing it.

She did it so good; I told her of course I would return the favor. But without protection it would have to be done later. So she went to the kitchen and returned within seconds with a small piece of plastic wrap. Then she laid on her back and gapped her legs and said, "Use this to protect you from my creamy glaze."

Then I applied the dental dam and bam... she was like purrin' and shit, as I hit the clit, I was killin' it.... orally... she was like "Aye Poppie"!

After she released my ears, I got up and took a swig of my beer, which was on the counter; where I proceeded to mount her. And we did it and did it and we did it; and we did it and did it, and we did it until, I finally had to say, "Quit it!" Hell, I couldn't continue I had to admit it.

She, fucked the shit, out of me.

As far as rendezvous, that was our only one. But now that was the most fun I ever had with plastic wrap and a condom. My thoughts are often of her; I wonder if she feels the same. I know I'll always remember that night of protection, passion and Mary Jane."

Geechie Woman

BY *Credence Malone*

Being with him is
like slipping into a new satin dress
and walking into church
when you know you've been a saint all week
Nose high in the air, no despair
Comfortable in your decision to be there

Sliding across my naked flesh
like a satin sheet is his love
His breath on my face,
Freshness in the gettin' up morning
He tends to my garden with ease and conviction
His attention, my pleasure
Like Southern breakfast perfection

Like taking the bacon off just in time to toss the eggs
and stirring the grits onto a plate
So that in exactly 30 seconds they will cool and take shape
Like the butter on top of them melting into a pool
Running into tiny rivers that trail artistically onto the plate
Like steaming apples crystallizing on hot cakes...

He fits my body like a Southern meal
Prepared with two parts love
and two parts skill

He washes his hands before he sits down at my table
always giving thanks and praise every place praises are due
But I can tell, while though I serve it well
I have prepared for him, all that I am able
A well traveled Southern gentleman
with a palate for many flavors
I suspect there is something new he savors

I've never been the type of woman
Who would resort to drastic tactics to keep a lover
But lately my heart and my head are engaged in riot
and I just can not fight it,
This urge to invest red sauce in his diet to make him true
I feel like a Geechie woman gone mad
Tell me ancestors

Stranger Let's Talk

BY *Jessica Holter*

He was the blackest man glowing like passion speaking through the darkest night. And as I kneeled at my bed's heel to pray I could feel his coal black eyes burning through my backside. We had left the club together; me and this man I didn't know. Now he was at my place, accepting an open invitation into my space. We both knew why we were here, so I thought I'd cut to the chase, erase any confusion, combat any illusion that he might have about my sexual deviance or carelessness. So at the risk of his leaving I began speaking, "Hey stranger, let's talk."

"I don't want to talk to you," he said. "I just I want to touch you. You know your body's aching for me to love you."

"You can love me right if you strap up tight. I got my condoms in this basket, you can see them if you turn on the light."

"We don't need no light and I don't want a rubber, see your body's wet and I am hard as lumber. I can't feel the wetness of your kitty cat if my rod's got to wear a hat." He spoke authoritatively through thick lips as he grabbed my hips and placed me on his lap. His eyes accentuated exaggerated movements across my flesh, just as his feet had on the dance floor. I wanted so much more. I was drowning in a stew of emotion, fear lashing at my face, with the force of a stormy ocean as his hands slithered like snakes toward prey across my shaking frame. I didn't even know his name.

"Hey stranger, we need to talk."

"You start talkin', I'll get to walking, I ain't here to play."

Filled with dread my mind was twisted as passion reared its deceptive head. My brain was speaking but its sounds were leaking through the springs of long too empty a bed. Black as the night that consumed us, he stood like a god chiseled from ebony. Life is spoiled when nature's disloyal. I was caught up in black as the moonlight gleamed off his bulging pecks and rode the curves of his six-pack. His muscles were engraved with veins, intensifying his rare frame. Yet the natural light did not reveal his drug tracks. I was smitten by yearning, craving that got fires burning when my body began whispering lies to my brain. The smart me, inside of me that had, heretofore, kept the flames at bay, just sat back and began to pray.

"Stranger, Let's Talk." I was caught in his embrace, looking into his face, without seeing, talking gibberish, not waiting long enough for answers to questions that balanced on a fine shuddering life line. "Don't you think we should talk?" My voice was uttering uncertainty, weakly giving in to his need to run this thing.

"You like the way I move," he said, "is that what you want to talk about?"

How I want to kiss your mouth or how I'll go south to visit your, love exquisite. Or how your heart races, running toward me. Or what perfection be like, when we be one. Stop your quibbling I feel you shivering longing to be fed. You start first and give me head. You're causing a ruckus for no reason at all, when all you really want to do is suck this. He readied himself for oral injection stroking his tool with arrogance. My mouth was ajar as my soul began to spar with insult, intrigue and flagrancy. The fire within dimmed to a slow simmer as I stared blankly at his offering.

Black, almost purple, it was hard for only me. He said, as my mind read lies in his eyes. For a fleeting moment I could hear the sermon old Pastor Carey used to say. And I could feel my bed of betrayal roll from the stranger's weight; his hands began to grope as the preacher man, in my head, spoke...

"Can't you hear death croon,
outside the upper room.
Can't see Jesus answer,
Father if it is your will,
I will, die on Calvary hill.
Can't you see him struggling
with the weight of the cross?
Yet the savior's saving souls
of, sinners lost.
And as they pierced hands
and then they pierced his feet,
I can I hear the voice of my,
Jesus speak,
"This night, not tomorrow,
I will end your sorrow."

The thief looked into the teacher's eyes,
and saw himself in a heaven paradise.
I hear the voice of my rock calling saying
Pastor Carey,
preach when they want to hear it
and, hah, preach when they don't want to hear it.
See, as death was knocking,
mother earth was rockin' like a
drunk man wobbling
and the sun — refused to shine.
Cause the S.U.N.
and the S.O.N.
couldn't shine at the same time.
Y'all don't hear me though.
Said the grave couldn't hold him
and the earth couldn't take him

cause the Father of the Trinity
could not forsake him......

I smiled at the vision in my mind and I opened my eyes
to see that old thief come back like a saint standing in my
window replacing the moon's glow with his own. "Child," he
said simply, "God knows you're not the only woman who is
lonely tonight. Wait for his storehouse of blessings to rain on
you and wash away your pain. It's not your time to go." He
vanished leaving abundant light that flooded my place and
I could see the needle marks trace, up the stranger, scaling his
arms and his dancing feet.

"Mister Night Club Dancer, Mister Heart Romancer, Stranger,
get up from your seat. You will not talk but you will listen: Killer
man your ass I'm dismissing. My spirit was dead but now it's
awake, like the thief come from the stake to heaven's gate. My
life you will not take. You see I ain't Jesus and my death won't
free but one soul. Mister hype head, you must want to see me
dead. Leave now or I'll see you in a casket. My finger itched on
the trigger of the gun I'd pulled from beneath my condom
basket. You want to be my lover without a rubber; I should
shoot you now for thinking it. Get up now, Mister Stranger, just
go, cause tonight you won't be freaking it."

Punany Dream

BY *Jessica Holter*

I want to lick your jimmy
until it's slick with my spit
cum all over you as you ride this
Heavenly split
Listen to the body as its waves we the path
to the G Spot you hit
I pay tribute to the master
Who does not miss my clit
Like fire spreading hot and wide
I will ingest you daddy as you confide
Delivering you from the struggle on the streets outside
The window of my soul is encased
In my eyes
But the window
Unveiling passion hides deep inside
Can you reach it
Stimulate it
Taste of its cream
Dig deep, deep
Deeper still
The thought of you is making me scream

With the certainty of fire and ice
I beseech you
My brother fill
This body I offer
A living sacrifice
To the black man I have known
All my life
Daddy
Lover
Provider supreme
While you're working tonight
My realizer of dreams
Why don't you dream
On this body and these
Punany scenes

Mind Fuck

BY *J Steal*

The night has stolen your sleep
It's morning
Sista you look kind of tight.
Is that the weight of the world
you are wearing?
Take it off.
Take it all off.

Don't watch the clock
We will set time off course
Let me slide some oil
down the curve of your mind
and find heaven,
amidst your forsaken dreams
for family, for labor, for life
We will take the time to love,
Take the time to give,
take the time to chill,
We will take time and
bend her selfishness to our will.

There is no night, no noon, no day
no seconds, minutes, no hours
Only us
Objects of two souls' desires
There will be no protection necessary
as we shall neither, kiss, lick or suck
My desire is to become infected with
Your Story, Your Energy, Your Love
Tonight, my darling, we will mind fuck.
Tell me of your fears
Tell me of your heaviness
Speak to me, of your passion
Reveal to me, your heart

And if you feel the need to cry,
Let the wetness flow
upon my strong hands
For I am more than your lover
I am a man

and when time finds her way back to the world,
our minds will be climaxing

Microbicides are **products** such as gels, **creams** or intra-vaginal rings that could be **applied topically** to the vagina, **reducing transmission** of HIV during **sexual intercourse.** Microbicides are still in development.

Ain't I a Man?

BY *J Steal*

I bring her flowers...
She turns from the
blossoming possibilities
of becoming victim
of a tender touch
a gentle whisper
a stroke
that has been softened
by all that this man's eyes have seen.

Does not the boy
who wipes tears
from the eyes
of women warriors
crushed under penal codes
grow to be a man?

If only she could
surrender
to the femininity in me

Submit
to the thrust of throbbing energy
that is the making of
not just the muscles
of my ass and thighs
But of the power inside

The Goddess and I,
her loyal servant
sent to her scent
like a honey bee
it is Spring
and there is much work
to be done

She turns away from the
blossoming possibilities
of love.

She spits petals of venom
"His hands are not rough enough"
"His voice is not harsh enough"
to tame the shell shocked
Prisoner of War
she has become

Her eyes are empty caverns
robbed of soul

Even if I took her now
ravished her
until respected me
The union would only
shame the Gods
For she is but a fraction
of what was once whole

Some day soon
she will open
her swollen eyes
and cry
"Now there was a man.
Why ain't he mine?"

Destiny's Dance

BY *Jane Therese*

Listen to my soulful prose
As your tongue rolls
Over vanilla-flavored safety
From my sugar glazing holes
First your greeting
Salivating, eating
I can see our bodies meeting
Time is fleeting
Take me now
I wonder how
You can sit there
Mesmerized
And hypnotized
Your Jones arise
Free you from your chains
I want you unrestrained
You go insane
Your body drains
You can not hide it
Can not fight it
I want to ride it

You got the glove
I got the love

When you are weak
I'll make you strong
I want to love you hard and long
With saccharine kisses
You can't miss this
I wanna hold you
Want to fold you
Can I mold you?
Where you fit
In my shrine of forgiveness

Can't you feel this warm retreat
From the evil, from the killers
From the liars in the street?
I wanna give me to you sweetly
Yes I know boy how to treat thee
When you were here, I was coy
Now that you're gone boy, I want more
This body throbs with steaming heat
Me and you no greater feat
Merge with me
Till we're complete
Images so very sweet
Got me sliding off this seat

Take me in the bathroom
On the sink and on the floor
Lay me in the bedroom
On the bed and on the dresser
Wrap my legs around your waist
As you enter my secret space
Fate's embrace
My fingers trace

Muscles of your body
Chestnut cast of your face
The fight is on but it can't erase
Your Nubian power, Your African Grace
Enter me with sweet perfection
Without a flinch, without a hitch
I accept your love injection

Drums resound
When you have found
In me a home
No more to roam
Can't you hear ancestors cry?
They don't want this love to die
I am nature
I am mother
I am woman
I am lover
Deliver you from life of game
Last night my prince
I saw your name
Etched in the headstone of a grave

These streets will kill you
I want to heal you
Have earned it
But don't you burn it
Strap up in this cock pit

Grab a hold on Destiny's hands
Do a strong and rhythmic dance
Bathe in my body's water
Oh boy it's getting harder
To control my longing soul

Feel the cadence of my light
I do promise fiery flight
Won't you use your third sight
To see my purpose is to give
This Destiny Dance
Is life everlasting
In me,
Black man, live

Pussy Talk

BY *Ghetto Girl Blue*

My pussy talks way too much.
She's a vulgar little fucker at that.

I mean, just when I get to wondering
where all the good men are,
I see a one, at least I could hope

We get to talkin' about
My hopes, my aspirations,
His plans and dreams
It's going real well until
My pussy gets that nagging twitch
Like she just can't hold a thing
Swelling to tell my secrets
She blurts a dripping question
As to the stiffness of his dick

I shuffle my legs gently back and forth
Thinking "Sshh, down girl!
Don't fuck this one up!"

Hop up on the barstool, cross my legs,
Press her lips together

"Shut the fuck up!"
But since she wasn't wearing anything,
feeling way too free...
When the music stopped
She mumbled something freaky
and began to drool
Her voice, as vulgar as she intended it to be
Sticky with wine
and muffled by thighs
Crept up on me like a thief
Then called me out like a whore in the street

"Don't sweat it, baby," the man said.
"he Lady know what she wants."

My Pussy and him got along great
But I didn't like him much.
He made animal sounds. He fucked like a beast.

I walked on all aching fours out of the hotel room
Low. I made her promise not to get in my business again
She said she would.

But she didn't stop until I was married.

Swell of Tear

BY

I watch
In your slumber

I want
To rob you from sleep

I fear
The recoil of your flesh

I mourn
The death of your touch

I lay
In the empty place

I exist
Between your thin breaths

I pine
To feel your words caress me

I throb
In the remembrance of lust fulfilled

I thirst
For your baptismal waters

I swell
In a well of tears

I come
Into a silent space

I wash
Before you awake

Although researchers have found HIV in the saliva of infected people, there is **no evidence that the virus is spread by contact with saliva.** The lining of the mouth, however, can be infected by HIV, and instances of **HIV transmission** through oral intercourse have been reported.

—National Institutes of Health and Human Services

Sweating the Tears of Sappho

BY *T. Calloway*

I drove by your ex-girlfriend's house last night, saw your car, paused to contemplate a jealous rage but kept driving. I really didn't have plans to do what I did and it didn't just happen. It was destiny. She unveiled herself slowly over the months before, but now her message to me is undeniable and she was working, even through you, to help me see my way clear from this lie we call a relationship.

It was something in your kiss, you see. Something in your taste, that was all too familiar to me, when you strained to bend your lips to me on your way in the other night. You tasted the way you tasted when I found you. So I put 1 and 2 together, me on this lonely naked street and you... and your beautiful face cradled in the warmth of her ample hips and got a hypotenuse triangle in which the sum of the square of this long lasting love you have for her is equal to the length of my unrest; squared.

My eyes welled with tears and I could barely see, as I drove away. But my ears engulfed the urgent wail of Johnnie Taylor's promise that all is not lost for a wondering soul of the night, dismissed from life as she new it: A compromising place where the straight play with their soul's salvation. Our room.

Where there is only a bed and the lasting resonance of the piercing sounds of my surrender to your tongue. Unwavering shards of girl on girl passion. Unforgiving truth. An uncompromising heat sleeps with me. I sweat the tears of Sappho. Me and the Goddess up against the world and its hypocrisy – a hot seat that gives my skin an anxious itch.

My car pulled to an impatient stop as that Taurus talked turkey.

"Now who's making love to your old lady
While you were out making love?
Who's making love to your old lady
While you were out making love?"

And just like that, my heart was washed clean of anxiety and flushed with the anticipation of revenge; the Scorpio cure, as I pulled down the visor, touched up my mascara, and hypnotized myself.

"Damn, I looked good," I said out loud, just to make sure you weren't still caught in my throat.

"What was she thinking"? I spoke again as I stepped from the car. My voice was soothing and deep with that seductive kind of pain born of American blues as, for a moment, I pictured you with your mouth on her. I, myself, tasting her again, I convinced myself to stay angry enough to go through with this. Reminding myself that this was to me more than an affair, but a change

I channel the fever into fervor, using the intensity for the long walk up the path that lay ahead of me. I hadn't worn those red stilettos in far too long. A gust of wind swept beneath me lifting the hem of my swing coat, and with a cool fingertip, touched my naked Punany and felt her blush.

When I rang the doorbell, he fell running to it and knocked over the umbrella stand when he hugged me. Now I blushed, remembering men and their natural response to me. The utter suspension of their intelligence at the mere promise of Punany is blinding. I could barely see you anymore, even in my mind.

While, for lesbians, there really is no mystery. You bleed, I bleed and we try not to kill each other in between.

He played a song for me on his baby grand, and did a little tap dance while he rolled sushi and fried tempura vegetables. He made a jingle of my name and clicked his heels in mid air. We Orbitzed together and booked that little trip to Vegas I've been bugging you about. You know the one you put a deposit on and just couldn't make that last payment on?

...and for a while, in his bed, I dismissed my hang-ups, let my father lay quiet in his grave. Surrendered completely to natural love, the way my mother taught me it was intended to be. He milked the poisonous venom of rejection from every part of me and from my mouth came only sweetness, for a good change.

I awoke, just hours before the police retreated from the streets and skies. Every muscle aching, even the hair on my head rejuvenated, my skin ... a natural glow that does not come in one of those bottles my skin has been obsessing over.

It was nearly 5 in the morning when I returned home. You did not stir as I showered, put on my pajamas, top and bottom, and slid between the sheets.

You had not even noticed I was gone. But I am.

Sweet Confection

BY *T. Calloway*

I have a confession
You have become my obsession
You made such an impression
On my sweet confection

Let me reciprocate
Lubricate your ear holes
Punctuate the recall with my poems
Erotic memories,
Biting gently on your lobes

Lay your body down, you said
Forget all the troubles of this world
Let your love unfurl, you said
Don't undress, just rest, you said
and spread, I did

Not by the power of your hand, but by
The urgency of your breath and tongue
We were one, you dined
Penetration
Being furthest from your mind

You are a goddess
Mother of the Sun, you said
Your womb calls to me
Your sweetness is sublime, you said
Don't hold back from me,
I am thirsty
Let yourself come into the heat of my breath, you begged

Time has no power in your bed,
Release, give it up, you said
Fade into the blackness of the night,
Feel nothing but my tongue,
Become nothing but the throbbing pulse,
beating the walls of your heart down, you commanded
Your oral muscle to thrash against the shores of my temple
Get lost in the crash, dirty dance with me, you said
Hold me ears, Fuck my face, you said
Come baby, come baby, baby come
I did

My body wracked with spasms,
My pelvis mindlessly pumped against the energy between us
I temporarily forgot to breathe, my eyes searched for my brain,
out of focus, like hocus pocus
my skin came alive, feet tingled, stiffened
a beat, expanding and contracting rhythmically
rising and falling at the call of the gravitational pull of your tongue
a tidal wave of sensory perception, a spot of G softening
to your touch...
you are a milky moon, you said, now cum
I did.

My Invisible Man

BY *Dayna Gaspard*

I remember when his eyes would follow me.
He watched me move.
Watched my large long hands flip through his CD's
"You have so many," I whispered.
Every R & B and Hip Hop offering was stacked neatly
on his mantle.
His Mantle. I sighed, everything her is his.

With my back to him,
I knew this would be the last time I would touch all that was his.
He spoke slow and deliberate into the phone.
Interested, Engaged. A tone no longer found in his
conversations with me.
I usually flutter through his condo—ignoring him—
more interested in
his pet snake, or painting my toe nails.
That evening—not feeling his large black eyes burn into my skin—
I was desperate.
I shook off my fear and focused on seducing him.
Seated comfortably in his leather arm chair,
he cradled the phone on his shoulder
while rolling a joint on his lap.

He glanced at me, then laughed hysterically into the phone.

My heart fell between my legs and bounced against the floor.
I slowly crawled towards him,
across his thick white shaggy carpet.
On hands and knees,
my bra-less breasts bulged from my tank top
and my tight mini skirt rolled up my thighs.
Me the awkward lamb, posing as a prowling tigress.
With every forward motion, I was pushing, probing,
and forcing a reaction.
Demanding his affection. Still on my knees, I sat by his side
like those obedient fancy French poodles.

He stroked my hair and rubbed the back of my neck.
Resting my head against his jeans—my face burned with shame.

He sucked his teeth, which meant he would smile that end-
less crooked smile. He was satisfied that I was on my knees.
"Hey, uh, go upstairs and get ready for bed," he mumbled,
now squeezing the back of my neck.
Like a little girl I obeyed my fading lover.
In his bathroom, I lathered up my pussy real good, removing
all traces of that salty, clammy taste.
I put on the fresh lace panties from my purse and slid
between his satiny sheets.
I woke hours later to his phone ringing—the clock said 3:15.
Hey lay on top of the covers, knocked out snoring with weed
and pussy on his breath.
The phone stopped, then started ringing again.
Sharp pains ran through my body—
I felt pressure behind my eyes.
He struggled around for the phone—a woman—
only a woman would call this late
a woman he was fucking.

Before my eyes his dark smooth skin turned translucent
My eyes burned as I gathered my clothing
As my legs moved my body through what was his
I felt his presence, I mean his very being, slowly disintegrate
around me
just fade away

Daddy Sam

BY *Jessica Holter*

You wanna know why I fuck, old man?
Why your welfare check
should feed my seed?
My children are the spoils
of the war you wage
against my lovers
as they run
through the front door
Stop.
Fuck.
Long, hard, strong,
Sweetly, goodly, Godly

You ever been fucked by a Black man?
It's something indeed Daddy Sam

Way off in the middle of the gun-ridden night
where silence is imaginary
and freedom is a joke
That old slave come running
to my door

Broken, weary, worn
Flesh torn, unhealed
His body collapses
as my arms fold 'round him
His mind still races, running,
seeking soft wet places
To wash away his pain

You ever hold a Black man?
It's something to feel Daddy Sam

My urban tongue is sharper than a two-edged sword
My head rolls, my eyes, they flash and bat
My arms fold, like a shield
Across my breasts
Protecting the heart
Which has never known the freedom to care
to truly care for this Black man
the one who is dead yet alive
But something deep inside of me,
Deeper than pain, deeper than grief
deeper than our struggle
Bubbles up, threatening to overflow me
Like a volcanic eruption
When I see into his bloodshot eyes

You ever look into the eyes of a Black Man?
They will consume you Daddy Sam

All at once I submit
To some ancient desire
To be a woman
To run free and dance on the shores
of a homeland I have never known
Tantalizing this man while he watches
The thrusts and gyrations of my temple
A feast for Kings lay before him

Breaking bread, devouring fruits, juice drips
from his lips
tantalizingly, invitingly, promising me
He sits
On a sandy beach,
land neither he nor I have ever known
Yet it thrives in my mind
He has worked all day
On land that is his
And has earned a right to this feast
and to feast on this, my dancing sanctuary
My carnal desire washing over him
waves from this vast ocean
Called a Black woman's soul

You ever connect with the soul of a Black Man?
It's proof of heaven Daddy Sam

I give to him, what I have to offer
and watch him eat as I rub his feet
They soak in a pail of water and suds
I stand before him and unleash my robe
Aggressively, deliberately
The way I feel tonight!
Down on my knees I grab a foot from the pail
His toes trail, water from
my lips, down my neck
to my rising cinnamon nipples
Tracing the pattern of his seal
emblazoned on my belly
The scars, he says, of a "real woman"
I laugh because his words tickle
and jump as his toes play
In my shrine of generation

You ever seen the relaxation of a Black Man?
It's a rare occasion Daddy Sam

So I,
give it to him like fire and ice
No doubt.
He does not have to guess
His dick talks to me
and I know his pleasure...

I have scaled the pained walls of time
to be in the place, in this moment
Facing his desire to be inside of me
I am hot, I am throbbing, I am wet, I am ready
I thirst to feed, I give to drink,
from the rivers
that flow beneath my surface
I
am the earth's crust
He is a majestic Mahogany tree trunk
whose frilly branches and leaves
Have fallen off in stormy weather,
yet his roots remain
firmly embedded in me
I bathe in the light of his strength
and marvel at the thickness of him
as he burst through me,
Forging for the heat
of my pulsating core

You ever succumb to a Black Man?
A gentile warrior needs willing prey Daddy Sam

Now it may seem crude
To speak of loving as a fuck
But then, love, real love
Wholesome love, honest love, responsible love...

Extends from the kitchen to the board room
It is an unyielding need to keep your family fed
Keep a roof over their heads
Just as my babies grow inside of me,
The provider grows inside a man.
But that soil he is planted in, must be
fertile soil.

How can a Black man
Promise passionate retreat
from these cruel, cruel ghetto streets
While gazing into my eyes
and kissing my lips
while caressing my skin
and eat
of my pussy
When he cannot feed
my children?
I ain't had good loving
Since before the rocky ride
On the rippled waters of
the Atlantic

You ever recall the voyage of the Black Man?
He is reminded every day Daddy Sam

He is reminded at work
He is reminded in stores
He is reminded on the streets
while trying to hail a taxi cab
He is reminded while driving Black
I could go on and on
But the one place he will never be reminded
of his shackles
is between my loving arms

That is why this welfare girl is here
Every day, or even
every now and then
To offer this body
for what ever its worth
A living sacrifice
or just a romp to ignite old thrills
A slow run through Elysian fields
or just letting that old slave shuffle, duty free
in the nappy dug out
Every time my temple spills
Over the stiff, long, dark, hungry flesh of him,
I will think of you Daddy Sam
and try to make fertile soil
of the scraps,
that fall from your table

Question 22

BY *Kineta James*

Seem like I been here all day long. I came at 8:00,
cuz dat when they said to be in line
For what seem like days. Little Mookie crying and shit.
The cross-eyed bitch
across the room got one more time to look over here
like she wanna
tell my baby to shut up...
and where the hell is dat damn worker?
Fuck Big Mookie. I gotta always be up in here by myself
He wanna be the only one up in here by his self

(I grab my pussy and try to squeeze the itch away instead of
scratch.)

Thinking if Im'ma have enough time to pick up dem antibiotics
what Mookie say Im'ma need. I could kick dat crack ho's ass
for givin' Mookie some.... Where the fuck is dat worker

My pussy itch.

The pinching
ain't working
So I jis
press my lips against
Little Mookie stroller
'til that
cross-eyed bitch
had calt my name
all that fuckin'
time in line
just to get to
Question 22
Like cuz I'm broke
I can't have sex wit nobody
I'm like...
"No. I don't know who
Little Mookie daddy is."
"No, ain't no man livin wit me"
"No, I ain't got no jewelry I could sell"
"Hell yea! I want food stamps!"
and.... "Could you give me my Medic-aid today?"

Da Heat outside make my pussy itch worser
I be glad when Big Mookie could stop slanging,
get his rap thang on
A real job, so my pussy won't always have to be sick
from these desperate ass crack hoes and stuff

Damn, I shoulda got a bus pass hook up

It's hella hot

Sanctified and Satisfied

BY *T. Calloway*

"How you gon' get good lovin'
From a man you keep breakin' down?"
Oooh, he may be tired
Black men they do get tired
And oh, his soul may be crying
Fighting the 400-year fight
When he's feeling weary
Give him that sexual healing
And he will always stay

Sanctified and Satisfied
Strong and ready, to fight another day

And ooh he may be shamed
Black men they do feel shame
Knowing she doesn't see him
The way she used to see him
And no, she don't do him
Like she used to do him
Wash him in your sugar rain
One thousand and one different ways
And his soul will reverb

Sanctified and Satisfied
Strong and ready, to fight another day

He'll keep the food on the table
If you treat him like he's able
Girl, you've got to
Whisper to his body
That you ain't lost the faith
With all the skill those lips can
Over and over again
"He'll never be anything less than a man"
And he will rise

Sanctified and Satisfied
Strong and ready to fight another day

Never a Place to Fight

BY *D J Blackmon*

This place we rest
Where we taste moments of passion
See visions of happiness
In scented aromatherapy
By muted candlelight
Is always an arena for love and sex
But never a place to fight

This space where we take our repose
Let down our defenses
Remove all of our clothes
We fulfill each other's fantasies
And share each physical delight
A zone for us to express alone
But never a place to fight

This spot where we find satisfaction
Where we experiment with different things
To see each other's reaction
The pleasure each tickles brings
Reach new and different height
An area for new positions
But never a place to fight

This is the location where our peace resides
Where we escape from weariness
And seek shelter from where fear hides
In secret languages we speak of things
By signs in the middle of the night
In a room where plans for progress is meant
But never a place to fight

This dwelling of our hopes and dreams
Is never a place for shouts or screams
Where hands should caress and never be fisted
Where bodies are never bruised or blistered
Where mistakes and hurt are made alright
Because is a space to fix and erase
But never a place to fight

Risky Behavior

HIV can infect **anyone** who practices risky behaviors such as:
- **Sharing** drug needles or syringes
- **Engaging** in sexual activities while you are **high** on drugs or alcohol
- **impaired judgment**
- **Having sexual contact,** including oral, with an **infected person without using a condom** and using it correctly.
- **Having sexual contact** with **someone whose HIV status is not known to you**

A great way to **get safe** and **stay safe** is to **get tested** together and **remain monogamous.** —A.F.A.C.T.

Artists Fighting AIDS Creatively Through the Arts

Real Sex

BY *Kineta James*

Give me some light, so I can see
The image of our silhouettes dancing on the wall
Give me eternity, so we can be
The epitome of Real Sex while we ball

Hood rats they come and go
But you I know for sure
Got me from the back to the front to the middle
Just lay that ass on my pillow
Got your body shaking like Jell-O
I don't have real sex with hoes
But we'll play the parts as they go

My Negro, My Hero
Let down your platinum dick
We can role play all got damned day
I'll be the ho and you be the pimp
I'll be the doctor if you play sick
Lick it up, flip it baby slap it one time
and I'll be an S&M Chick

Hood rats they come and go
But you I know for sure
Got me from the back to the front to the middle
Just lay that ass on my pillow
Got your body shaking like Jell-O
I don't have real sex with hoes
But we'll play the parts as they go

Now Flex for Real Sex
You know, what comes next
My heart, your hand, my eyes, your mind,
my thighs, your back, my lips, your kiss, my ears, your tongue
my bed, your jeep, on land, or at sea, in the sky, it's a synch
I'm down for it all when it comes to ballin'
cuz I'm your # 1 bottom bitch

Quickie

BY *Branden M. Pernell*

We don't have much time.
In fact, only a few minutes X's two
But that's more than enough time
for us to do what we need to do.
Nah! Don't take off that skirt—just hike it to your waist—
Remember, time we can not waste.
Open your blouse just a little,
so I can suckle upon your nipples
While we discreetly do our love dance.
There's a chance, someone may discover our erotic scene,
So please don't scream,
Just slide your tongue in my ear (and gently wiggle)
while you work that thing.
When we've finished, I'll discard the used prophylactic,
Fasten my pants, and put on my suit jacket.
And you,
you'll put your breasts in your bra and fasten your blouse;
Primp your hair and check your compact to make sure
it's not too obvious
We just did that.

As you fix your skirt,
we compliment each other on our puttin in work.
As the elevator doors open, the scene we quickly flee,
and nobody's even knowin' about our little Quickie!

Jack

BY *Jessica Holter* AND *DJ Blackmon*

Run, Jack. Run!
Pack up your gun!
See Jack See
Pretty ain't always fun

Bill pimped nimble
Will was slick
Don't be too quick
To hit Jane with that stick.

You know Bill,
best friend to Will?
Always looking for a brand-new thrill

See, Bill met Jill
Up on that hill.
Cause he was looking for a hole to fill

Now, Jane and Jill,
They both know Will
But Will got clap from a girl named Camille

"Bill shot his gun"
Jane and Jill had their fun
Now Will ain't the only one
Burning like the sun

Trudy & Bill

BY *G. T. McCoy*

Trudy and Bill went over the hill
They wanted to have a time that was nice

Trudy said, "Look here, Bill, If you want somma
my thrill, you gotta go down not once, but twice."

Bill popped a grin, licked his lips and dived right on in
and did his duty with both relish and care

Trudy shook and she moaned, she wiggled and she groaned
She let out a whistle and says "Yea Bill! Yea! Right there!"

So Bill kept it goin' then gave a lick and a peck
Trudy finally let out a holler, twitched and 'bout broke poor
Bill's neck

Bill yells out, "One!"
Trudy whispers, "Baby you ain't but half done.
Don't forget you's got a long way to go."

Bill slips a smile, Teeth gleamin' like a crocodile,
Stretches his neck and says, "Trudy, yea, I know."

Bill got back to work. He real gentle but he still goin' berserk,
Servin' Trudy like a pitcher on the mound

Bill keep goin' like the Energizer bunny
Trudy stretch open her mouth but she don't make no sound

Bill lift up his head, see Trudy face, and yells out, "Two!"
Says, "Hey now Trudy, you know what time it is, You know
what I want to do!"

Bill start gettin' ready, cause by now he done got real uptight
Trudy yawns, closes her eyes, and says, "Bill, go home. I'm
tired. Goodnight."

When you **have sex** with one person without protection, it is as if you have **had sex with everyone** they have had sex with before you. The **virgin** who gives herself on the first night to a man who has made love to hundreds of people, has herself made love to **hundreds** of people because she is **exposed** to whatever communicable **diseases** (and energies) that he has been exposed to. — A.F.A.C.T.

Understudy Bitch

BY *Kineta James*

They call me that freaky bitch, That sneaky bitch
That sucked up, fucked up, Got the nerve to be stuck up bitch

My pussy's talking, baby
Let's have a conversation
Don't need no degradation
Ain't trying to raise a nation
Just want some skin relation

Cause I picks my dicks discreetly
Sucks my dicks so very sweetly
Fucks my dicks with thrustin' energy
While your bitch is popping out babies
Sweet Dick Daddy you can always page me

So keep your wife and that bullshit life
and I'll keep giving you fever
I know what they say, It don't bother me
Because
you can't make a wife a ho neither

Your girl is throwing shade
But me she can not fade
She's tired, she's running around
chasing children 'round the playground
looking tore up, from the floor up
But me? I stays down like to flats on a dump truck
clean, groomed & ready to fuck

My pussy's talking, baby
Let's have a conversation
Don't need no degradation
Ain't trying to raise a nation
Just want some skin relation

So if your wife's got a problem with it
Tell her I'm here to fix it
Dial 1 800 Call a Ho
Cause there are some things
she needs to understand
Why I been fucking your man?
Because you ain't.
Because I can.
Because I'm selfish
I ain't took no vow to love, honor and cherish you
that shit is for him, and him alone to do
I'm fucking your man because the fucking is true
Hot, Nasty, Funky, Raw, Cussing, Lying, Sweaty, Cheating ass
Sex
feels so good 'cause it's so Taboo

Time's up, I gotta go
Gotta get my mane tamed
But I like you, so Im'ma give you some skin for the game
Don't be mad, don't pout,
don't even let him know that you found out
Inside, decide
if you even want his name

Outside, get on the upside
Dry your eyes, Get a babysitter
Wash your ass and watch your figure
Comb your hair, manicure, pedicure
Desirability is the master
if you're trying to keep the lying cheating ass bastard

One more thing, I know he's your husband
But he's only one of my lovers, so if I were you,
I wouldn't touch his dick without a rubber
to save my life

The Second Sin

BY *Ghetto Girl Blue*

So,
I heard you had a sweet tooth.
You are a health-conscious
Hard-working
Loyal Black Man
In need of a natural Black chick
One who is 100% freak
with no preservatives necessary
as my contents were designed
for immediate consumption

See,
Beneath this world
of war and destruction
there is but one remedy
my pussy.
She being the very essence of me
I am compelled by nature's command
to wash you sins away with the blood that flows within me

But first,
let me tell you what she needs.

She needs a man
who is stained with her scent
tongue and soul
As down to work for the good of his family
as he is to fuck
So confident is he
that he never needs to
feed from the scraps of any man's table
whether he be white or black

For the foundation of his story is built
Not in the shame of slavery
but in the healing power of the stripes on his back
The fabric of his life is woven
with his unspoiled semen

You are the weakness in my knees
The knowledge in God's forbidden trees
You are the song my pussy sings
When my sugar walls
sweeten your tongue
I want to hear the ancestors cry
"Let freedom ring."

It is no accident
the way my love fits your dick
for though we are heaven bound
our fucking is hell sent
for my one true heart burns like fire and brimstone
at the mere thought of your touch
If heaven is a place of purity and light
I will forever close my eyes
to her hypocritical lies

For no righteous deity
could ever conceive of mortal man
the conviction to abstain
from the sobering potion
that burns like hell fire
between my thighs

See with your mouth
not with your eyes

Take a forbidden bite
of nature's ripest fruit...
between my thighs

Multiple Touch

BY *DJ Blackmon*

The same arm
the same hand
The exact same face
of the very same man
And yet...
> He had a multiple touch.

The first, had to fathom
a soft caress, a ripple like the ultimate orgasm
mesmerizing as it traveled the length of my skin
absorbing the essence of my energy, taking all of me in
But then...
> He had a multiple touch.

The second, was steady and stern
a teacher with magical lessons of life to learn
A firm grip, massaging away the tension
with every finger tip.
But don't trip ....
> He had a multiple touch.

The last, took me by surprise
Both widening and blackening the both of my eyes
Bruising my ego and my spirit along with my flesh
wreaking mental and emotional havoc as the surface
of my tender body and his knuckles mesh.

I wonder why it hurt me so much
After all I knew ....
        He had a multiple touch.

About 1/2 (one-half) of HIV-positive women are beaten by their lover or spouse.

—A.F.A.C.T.

Feet

BY *Credence Malone*

Sit yourself down
Rest your feet.
For the road is rough
and the day is long.
Hear them laugh with joy
in my hands
Drink of wine,
While they drink of Egyptian musk oil
Now let them dance in the air
Betwixt coils of incense and
Smokey Robinson Songs

There

BY *Credence Malone*

We did it.
Wo wcnt there.
To that place they talk against
To that place that ends relationships...
that place that stops hearts
kills spirits
breads fear
fuels hatred
tests boundaries
hurts
ends lives

I had been bad, often
You were strong, always
I needed to be punished
You were good at inflicting pain
you had seen how it was supposed to be done
I was your drunk father

slap me!
pull my hair
spit in my mouth
harder
faster
deeper
fuck me Daddy...
I am your bitch!

It began

We should stop
I may start to like this, you warned
I could not see your truth for mine

Soon, I could only cum this way

Violence is wet and messy
a flood of emotion that leaks everywhere
and drains everything

By the time the police were standing between us
our careers were on the line
our fetish, a freak show
our friends and family
stood in line for tickets
placing wagers
waiting for the bell to sound and signal
the next round

I looked in the mirror
and didn't recognize myself
with my scars on the surface

It was a twisted game of
the fittest's survival
I made you play with me
positioning you,
so that I could learn to fight back

But in the darkest hour you show me where gentle lives

inside, to the second knuckle
up and back
you manipulated the softest part of me
I melted
like molten lava in your hand
and relinquished control

We did it.
We went there
to the place that is hell for so many fallen lovers

But we survived it
learned forgiveness
the meaning of grace
and lived to love each other again
and to make love to each other
without crutches

She Says

BY *Ghetto Girl Blue*

She says she
Wants to be with him
Though, any man would do

First come, first served
The old adage still rings true

She says she needs her man to qualify her
Dignify her, magnify her
Would take a man who'd stand up tall
Or lay right down and die for her

She says she needs two loving arms
Around her even if it is a lie
She needs a man, who loves her so much
It spills through his fists uncontainable

She says it's just a bruise
And bruises they do fade

That he didn't mean it,
Wasn't trying to hurt her

Won't do it again,
that he cried when it was over

That he needs her to feel his pain,
... to know his shame

That it's just fear of losing her
That's driving him insane

She says its only pain
and pain, it does go away

What is more?

It makes

making up

Soooo good the next day

The next day...
She says...

Doin' Time

BY *J Steal*

There was a little girl, who had the body of a woman
Eyes so pure, and soul so deep, her love could keep me
comin'
When she spoke, her soul would glow
I just had to know, how she possessed me so
Maybe it was her pouting lips I admired
or the way her hips shook with hell's fire
Lord! Curse my desire, to be up inside her
This, little girl, with the body of a woman

I was a man without plans for my life
I ain't gon' lie, your honor
I wasn't trying to make her my wife
I wanted to forget all my sufferin'
Get me some good lovin'
Lose my sins in her sweet innocence
A blessing from God, of which I was not worthy

Now I'm doin time in an eight by ten wonderin'
if heaven will have mercy and let me in

She's got a body, tellin' me hell's on fire
Skin of sin that, burn the soul

Man would be willin' to go to jail fo'
I was blinded, by that sweet body
How could I have seen, she was only fifteen?

I gotta throw myself on the mercy of the court
Why don't you tell the bailiff to go get her
You'll understand why I got wit her
I swear, mister, I didn't hit her, I just kissed her, then I licked her
and to my lovin' she surrendered
It ain't my fault that she's a tender...
with the body of a woman
Guess that don't count for nothin

'cause I'm doin time in an eight by ten wonderin'
 if heaven will have mercy and let me in

She's got a body, tellin' me hell's on fire
Skin of sin that, burn the soul
Man would be willin' to go to jail fo'
I was blinded, by that sweet body
How could I have seen, she was only fifteen?

Shadowin' the Dark

BY *Jessica Holter*

Invisible man
Materializing, casts
Shadow on my bed

Doing Man's Work
BY *The Head Doctor*

OK ladies, we will begin this session on dick riding with my personal favorite woman-on-top position.

#1 Thunder Thighs: Stretch for this one. Find a clean place on the floor. Lay a blanket down if you prefer, but nothing too thick, and no pillows. Lay his naked body on the floor. I suggest you wear a robe, but make sure that he is not wearing any clothing (especially socks :-) Walk to the place where his head lay, your toes pointing to his shoulders. Let him lay for a moment looking up at you in silence. Look down at him. Kneel to kiss him on the forehead then stand up over his face, feet planted on opposite sides of his head. Put away all modesty, allowing him to see your fully exposed promise. Disrobe yourself, allowing your robe to drop like a curtain about his face. (Talk some shit to get yourself pumped, this is a rough ride, suggested only for women with strong thighs.) His discomfort is a plus and will prepare him mentally for full submission and increase your sense of power. Talk as you walk the length of his body until you are standing over his erect penis. Turn around to face him, still looking down, making strong eye contact. You want him to see your eyes, fear and anticipate your control. Plant your feet firmly on the floor on either side of him, a few inches from his hips. Slowly lower your body, keeping your back straight and your thighs pointed outward at 45-degree angles as you squat to receive him. Your pussy should be completely wet. As it makes contact with the penis, let only the tip inside at first, so that he can feel the contrast between the temperature of the room and the temperature of you, inside. Imagine your pussy is a mouth, playing with the head of a dick. In a rotating motion, grind on the head as if you were dancing. Make playful conversation, (quote a freaky song's lyrics or Punany poetry :), get him off guard, then drop... in one strong thrust onto the dick, allowing your pussy to engulf it in its entirety. (Careful, he may cum quickly.) If he doesn't, fuck him, using only your thigh muscles to elevate and lower your body onto his dick. It may burn your thighs, but it is the most exhilarating ride, and it's great exercise! Continue for as long as you can in this position... then switch...

#2 Butterfly Man: Some men may not be agreeable to this position, (I secretly call "Bitch Man"), but try it on him anyway, explaining that it is one of a few ways that a woman can achieve orgasm while on top, without having to manually use her fingers to manipulate her clitoris. If he is agreeable, lay him on the bed on his back. Kiss his feet to let him know you appreciate his submission. If he's ticklish it's OK, it will only cause him to further relax. After playing with him, grab his ankles and push them forward so that now his back is down but his knees are up. Crawl up to him on your knees, and kiss his knees, and his thighs, while gently spreading his knees apart. Getting a man to open his legs can prove a difficult task unless he is expecting some oral play, so engage him. Lick and suck the insides of his thighs, down to his groin, stretching your body out towards the foot of the bed. When your mouth arrives at his dick, kiss and lick it lightly, graze it gently with your teeth. As it hardens, swallow the head and suck for a while, but only long enough to ensure his desire is mounting.

All the while your goal is to get his legs apart, so be sure to fondle his balls, rolling them in your palm. Kiss and suck them while stroking his dick with your hand. To be in this position his legs will drop naturally open. If you are both agreeable, dive into a rim job and you will get not only full exposure, but you will also, find a softened man who will be a willing Butterfly Man for you. As he relaxes into his role, slide swiftly but smoothly up between his legs burying your face in his neck. Pull your legs up so that your pussy is open and above his dick to receive it, but keep your legs inside his thighs, and slide down onto his penis, closing your legs, so that his dick feels locked inside of you. In this position you will fuck with your breasts pressed and rubbing against his face and chest. With your pussy full of him and your labia massaging your clitoris you can come quickly to orgasm. Squeeze your legs together to tighten your grip so that he may feel your pulsating walls surrounding him.

#3 The Easy Rider: This is the woman-on-top riding standard, also known as "reverse missionary." For the Cowgirl who loves sex in the early hours, this is an easily achieved position to accomplish on a stiffened morning dick. As he lay on his back dreading the alarm of a new day at work, slide out of the bed into the bathroom to relieve you full bladder and freshen up. Upon returning to the bed, say good morning and climb on top of him, gently pushing his dick inside of you. Begin slowly so that he can feel the warmth of your just waking pussy, still hot and sticky from marinating overnight. To increase your pleasure, you may want to manipulate your clitoris with your fingers as you ride. You will feel him get increasingly harder inside of you as you fuck him. This is a sign to increase your pace, as he will be coming soon. As you get the first signs of his coming, a slight spurting pressure through the walls of his shaft, you may want to lean forward to assume the "Vixen Position" to be sure that you are not left alone to finish your orgasm with a vibrator after he has left for work.

#4 The Vixen Position: The Vixen is the woman who knows what she wants and exactly how to get it. From "The Easy Rider" position, simply lean forward, placing your breasts on his chest and pressing your clitoris against his hard groin so that you can grind on it as you fuck him. The Vixen Position offers all of the comforts of missionary lovemaking with none of the sacrifice. In this position you can hug, kiss, lick, breathe into each other's ears and talk in low whispers. This will resonate your deep passion, just as when he is on top. However, it is the Vixen who is in control, deciding the measure of how deep the dick will penetrate, how long or how short a time it is held inside, and she possesses, to some degree, the power to control her man's ejaculation. With the bodies pressed together in this way, the energy is intense and conclusive, leaving no room for question about the purpose of the union — A mutual climax is on the horizon.

#5 Sit & Spin: Danger Will Robinson! If you are not careful the Sit & Spin could injure you, but performing it gives an awesome rush... Like bungee jumping. To achieve the Sit & Spin you alternate from "Easy Rider" to "The Great Outdoors" without letting your man escape the warmth of your flower. Like the pussy, every dick is different. They vary not only in color, shape and size, but also in curvature. Some curve to the left, to the right, down and even up, and while you may feel comfortable in one position you may not feel comfortable in another, depending on size and curve. The Sit & Spin will test the feeling of his dick inside of you from at least 180 angles. This is an important issue when considering to engage in the Sit & Spin which is, actually more of a dick trick than a position, but when the fit is right, can be practiced many times in one rodeo session. This trick is easiest when you are on the floor. But chances are that you will already be on the bed. So, from the "Easy Rider Position" make sure his legs are flat on the bed and spread slightly apart. Now, one leg at a time, lift your knee off the bed, dropping your ass slightly so as not to lose your grip on his rod. Now your body weight is on your feet. Lifting one foot at a time, inch your way in a clockwise or counter clockwise motion as if you are a spinning top. When you reach his thigh, step over it. Continue, very slowly—your goal is not just to turn around but to feel the sensation as the flesh of your punany reacts to him at these various angles. Once your back is to him, you may want to adjust slightly to lock him into his new place. This is a perfect time for him to sit up, rub on your back, connect, while you work your way up to another ride.

#6 The Great Outdoors: Ode to The Great Outdoors! This is the perfect position for men, who have women who have great asses! This position is also effective for bonding after a fight and for fantasy fucking, since neither of you has to see the other's face. Women can enjoy this experience while distancing herself from the presence of her partner but still receiving pleasure. She can gaze upon pictures, into the horizon, through windows, or into a mirror to feed her sexual vanity. In this moment, her body is perfectly poised from all angles and she is moving as a wild animal in nature, unconfined, free to be, fucking beautiful. She straddles her man while facing away from him, pushing her pussy, at her own pace, into a seemingly unattached dick that faces toward her, digging only as deep as she commands. Then suddenly, she invites him into her The Great Outdoors. She lowers her head, turning to look back, gazing over her shoulder into her lover's eyes, as if she only just realized he was there. It is a look of lust and invitation. He accepts.

#7 The 3 Point Ride: The goal of The 3 Point Ride is to gain stimulation of all of your most sensitive vaginal areas at the same time: Your CLITORIS (the little button under the hood where the labia minora (inside lips) meet at the top of your pussy), your G-SPOT (the soft place at the top of the inside of your pussy about half a finger deep), & your CORE (your internal shaft and the back wall) all at the same time. To accomplish maximum pleasure in this woman-on-top position, choose a nice, comfortable chair to sit your man down in. Straddle him, inserting his penis inside. Rather than pumping up and down, ride in a back-and-forth rocking motion, arching your back so that your clitoris is pressed against his pelvis when you are forward and sliding the length of his dick as you press down and push back. To allow yourself to feel his fullness: the trick is pressing down and relaxing in a rhythmic pattern that will massage your inner walls while your muscles retract and release. Your body will be as a rocking pinnacle. In your back-most position you are open and allowing him to fully plunge into you, feeling the tip of his muscle on the very back wall of your halls, but take only what you can bear. The more you relax, the more you can bear. But as you rock forward, you gain strength. The natural tension required of your stomach, pelvis and thighs will give you the power you need to become the aggressor as you move closer to him. As you rock forward, begin to tilt your pelvis down, until you can feel the flesh of his skin on your clitoris. You may want to use you fingers to pull your lips open and expose your clitoris to his skin. You may begin to feel a pressure similar to the need to pee, but you don't have to pee. Just keep riding, arching your back at its smallest point, pushing hard into him when you are at his base, keeping a steady musical pace at first and then quickening as your desire to explode increases.

#8 Yawning: With your man still seated in his chair and you on his lap straddling him face-forward, lift your legs so that they are in the grooves of his bent arms—you are yawning with your legs open this way. In this position you can be helpless as a bird, allowing him to penetrate you to any degree that he chooses. To keep control from your top position, lace your hands under his arms and hold to his shoulders with your fingertips facing you. Use you arm muscles to pull your body up and down. You may also engage your muscle strength by holding to the arms of the chair, lifting and dropping your ass, guiding and directing the union from your top position. To submit... lean back, placing your hands on the floor beneath you, and you will find him submitting to your womanhood, as he leans into you. With his face on your stomach, he can smell the essence of you and hear the sounds of penetration.

#9 The Standing Ride: From the Yawning position allow him to stand, without letting you go. Wrap your legs around his waist, and lock them at the ankles. Hold the back of his neck until you find a good groove and stroke. Employ your thigh muscles to hold tight to his hips when you are ready to let your hands free. With him holding your waist, you are able to ride freely without hands. You may also continue to hold him by the shoulders or cling to his neck for support. When he is about to release, he may hold tightly to your back, hugging you. Hug him back and receive him, making sure that your bodies are well balanced so that his legs do not fail him.

#10 The Kegel Embrace: Cop a squat on his dick as he sits in a chair, on the bed or on the floor. Close your eyes and hold each other. Do not talk. Do not look. Just feel the energy traveling from your body to his, and his to yours. Soon you will begin to feel his dick jump. Respond only with your pussy, squeezing his dick while it is inside of you. Feel your pussy muscles, and they grip. Feel your gentleness as you submit. Feel his power soaring through you. Stay this way only for a few moments, but ending it before he gets fidgety. After your embrace, do not stand quickly. Slowly push his dick out of you, using only the muscles of your pussy, leaving him with fond memories of your sensitivity and your strength.

Kegel

BY *D J Blackmon*

It was years before I realized
A pussy had an exercise
So if you've lost your muscle tone
And it seems like wide open space
Instead of an erogenous zone

Then kegel, kegel, kegel, kegel

Over-stimulation got you wet and juicy
But childbirth and that big ole thang
Has got you feeling loosey goosey
Or muscles weak and you get a little trickle
When you cough or sneeze or get a tickle

Then kegel, kegel, kegel, kegel

Strengthen up those pelvic walls
So you can grip that dick
and squeeze those swinging balls
I promise that he won't ignore it
They even have a barbell for it

So kegel, kegel, kegel, kegel

Wanna make it like before?
'Cause you're not celibate anymore
Increase your orgasmic intensity
Or simply stop that trickling pee
Then daily you can do like me

And kegel, kegel, kegel

Next to Your Punany

BY *Kineta James*

If your punany came
and sat down next to you...

Would she be like
"Now Bitch...You know you need to quit doggin me!"

"Would she be like, girl, I ain't seen you in a long time!
How you been?"

When your pussy walks into the room,
would you have to open up the windows?
Let some air in?

Hey, what would she be wearing?

Would you be glad you kept your grandmother's
plastic couch covers when she sat down?

Would she be prim, proper, happy & bright,
intellectually stimulating you while you drink Evian,
and discuss your relationship in relation to raising a nation
of men who don't wear their pants like diapers
and reside in cribs and their mommas' houses
and daughters
who don't become mothers before they are tax payers...

or
Would your pussy kind of limp into your living room
slouching & scratching like a dope fiend
begging and trying to sell you a box of stolen maxi pads

If a friend came over while you were visiting with your punany
would you let them in? Or would you be embarrassed?
Or be like hell of excited like
"Oh my God, you have got to meet my pussy! She is so cute.
She's got these pouty lips and this wild red hair..."

If your pussy came and sat down next
to you right now,
would she expect a few apologies?

Would she want to beat your behind?
If she said
she came to tell you she was dying
do you know for sure that she would be lying?

Unpimpable

BY *Ghetto Girl Blue*

Unpimpable
because
I believe in The Dream
The Stuff Cinderella was weaned on
Looking for me a John Henry to lean on
and uphold
like the backbone
I am

Unpimpable
Like Malcolm and Martin
fully realized yet unhardened
for I see the green for the demon it is

The paper pimp feeds on insecurities
teaching you to be sheep in their school
scribbling ever-changing rules
on the fabric of your self esteem
then brand you with a scarlet
"F"
for Fool

Solution

BY *Kineta James*

He's my Daddy Type
Cause he found me
Before I was ripe
Turned me into a real woman
Despite all the hype about virtue

Opened me up
Body and soul
Till no other brother would do
Like my Daddy Type

Some Kind of Freudian hype
Got me feeling like
The more I love him
The more I love myself

I'm trying to keep up with all the love
And all the
Fortified game
He's filling me with

"Give up your love, girl
Without shame

Someday you'll make a name
For yourself
But until then
I've got the soulution to our
Financial destitution
Brothas will come
And they will surely go
Sex is only sex; don't try to make it love
When it's done
All you should be thinking of
Is how cash for ass
Will help you advance
To whatever level to which you aspire"
My daddy Type could always
Take a simple thing
And make it higher

Oh, how I admired
His wisdom!
I was his willing pupil
His dedicated victim
His subject to study and mold
Left no fantasies untold
No inch of my body unsold

This story is old
But still it's true
All I can do is tell it
So another child lover
Can recognize a daddy type before
It's everlasting too late

See my Daddy Type
Was a hype, a drug abuser, a user
A common needle pusher
Pushing me into the streets
To supply his habit

Every penny I was saving,
Every dream of havin' babies,
Every fantasy of moving
Away from these streets
Worked their way through his veins
with a little reality check
Payment for all the lives
He turned out I suppose
Or all the daughters
He turned into hoes
Guess it's how life goes
How could I know?
You reap what you sow
When I never had a
Real Daddy to teach me

A hot shot got my Daddy Type
Before the check was cashed
Now I have assumed his debt

People think I am wrong
For being true to the stroll
But I keep tellin' them
It's all I know

Despite the fact I got
AIDS
Game states

"You gotta Let a Ho

be a ho"

Ghetto Cinderella

BY *Ghetto Girl Blue*

Once upon the ghetto
A sharp-dressing
Promise-making
Fast-talking,
Street-walking,
Night-crawling
Negro rested

Suspended by
The short stretch of time
Between schemes
and big-money dreams
On the throne of my mind

His cash was long
His game was strong
His hustle was on
I couldn't go wrong
I'm a Ghetto Cinderella
And this is my song

Give you to me, little girl
I will change your
Ghetto world

From rags to riches
Drop all my bitches
Dressed so fine
His words spilled like wine
I knew he was mine
Came down on him like
Hot sunshine

I did give
and Passion did live,
If only for a little while

This ghetto femme fatale
Would walk a country mile
To wear the Gucci style
for my mirror did behold
Fine jewelry,
expensive clothes
While caught in my folds
the cash did roll

How could it be?
I didn't see
My King,
become pimp
buying pieces of my soul?

I'm a Ghetto Cinderella,
my soul was all I owned

Intoxicated by his words
It was absurd
I couldn't have heard
My own
Sweet Mother's call
"Listen young queen as
Ancestral hands fall
The beat of the drum
grows tall!

Dance with the Lord
between heaven's walls,
Man can't give you it all!"

Telling how brothers ball,
how they make cash roll

that game is sold...

Not told.

In time Passion fleeted
and I was greeted
by Greed's unchanging hand

No one could understand
My erotic plan
To use sunshine pussy,
to help my man

Stress was mounting
when cash was in drought
But I wasn't doubting
just sat there pouting
when he brought a new queen
To our throne

"We can't do it alone,
the money is wrong
and your sunshine stuff ain't enough!"
Ass so soft,
he called her Puff

She and I worked the same track

But times remained tough
So he got rough
When I resisted
His hands were fisted
Crushing my face and
my Spirit with it

I'm a Ghetto Cinderella
and I just gotta tell you, I
got no more soul left to sell

Don't know how I missed it,
that snake in his eyes

Guess I was hypnotized
Surprised by my demise
raining down
I was ...
a clown

Dressed for this occasion
with designer persuasion

In a bad situation...

No room left for sorrow
Oh, mamma! I'm gonna,
Die tomorrow

Could you
save this sex slave
A small grave
next to yours so we can again
Dance
Dance
Dance

Dance with me Momma

To the driven beat
of drums in a
Ghetto Heaven
        Ghetto Heaven
                Ghetto Heaven

1000 Thread Count
BY *Ghetto Girl Blue*

We walk the stroll
where others dare not go
the nasty little truth about man
leaves a bitter residue
in packages for the trash can

Sister, don't hate me
appreciate me for
the answers you seek are mine alone to speak
and your ears are burning to know
why he treats you so

though you have chosen his bed.

He is master there
so you can not despair
when it is you who does not
hasten to let down your hair!

I take my chances
and accept the answers, win or lose
a whore is as a whore does
and you spread for brand-new shoes

Does it make you better
to lay for physical pleasure?
Mind bound by fitted sheets
1000 thread count
how deeply you must slumber!

The cost of complacency, independence
The cost of independence, loneliness

The independence he gains by stepping out on you
the complacent fool he can be with me,
priceless baby

Perhaps we both have roles in this dreamy life
where heaven and hell are indistinguishable fires
angels become demons, demons angels
as we bend truth for the sake of
our selfish, sinful desires

I will remind him of the burning flames
so that he may know
that heaven's at home

You just take care
that the sheets are not still on the line
when he gets there

The Perfect Wife

BY *D J Blackmon*

Each day I awaken to a warm familiar scene
A house that's filled with comfort, that's organized and clean.
I rise to make the breakfast, bathe the babies,
without a sigh or moan
And I don't mind the fact that it's a job I've taken on alone.
I do what's necessary, giving all that I have to give
I do all the things it takes, to insure I have a happy place to live.

But I've begun to dread the coming of night for though
I love my husband much,
I find I'd rather cook and clean than bear the violation
of his touch.
In the day, I dutifully accept his kisses, when deep inside,
I accept his tongue with dread
And my body becomes an empty shell that acquiesces
at night with him in bed.
I sleep with fitful dreams filled with hurtful things I cannot say
And wake happy to make his house,
a place he likes to return to every day.

I don't know how much longer I can pretend,
or how much more I can bear
It seems to be much easier at home
when my husband isn't there
The company of my girlfriends,
seems a better source of pleasure
Than any kiss or touch from him
that I've received in any measure
I don't know how to change the direction of my desire,
or to fix the turmoil in my life
But until then I'll continue to pretend and be the perfect wife.

Work

BY *Kineta James*

He work
cuz
she be work
It hurt
some time
She worth
the price
he pay
with
overtime
constructing
monuments
on the playground
of her trade
she work
in broad day
light
he take
lunch break
in shade

she work

he work

cuz
she be work

"A Comparison of Pimps and Batterers" by Evelina Giobbe

A woman is being **pimped** by a man when their relationship is contingent on her engaging in **prostitution** and **relinquishing** all or part of her earnings to him. The **relationship** is defined and **controlled** by the pimp for his economic gain. Since he typically **appropriates** all of the woman's money and she receives only "non-negotiable goods" in return, the woman becomes financially dependent on him and **unable to save** for an independent future. This is particularly true of a woman who is paid with crack cocaine **in lieu of cash**, which **prevents** her from purchasing basic necessities such as food or clothing.

For more information on Prostitution visit www.prostitutionresearch.com online

Momma's Lil' Baby

BY *DJ Blackmon*

momma's little baby love hoin', hoin'
momma's little baby love strollin' tracks
momma's little baby love strollin' strollin'
momma's little baby ain't neva' comin' back

so now you done got clean, you wanna save me?
you wasn't here when he said, he had love fa me
where was you back den?
where was that pie in'na sky hymn i thought i rememba'd
you sing?
befo dem pipe dreams read us a never-ending story
like dem Bible people, what neva did begat a clue
hard times had me missin' you and findin you in him

he said he would die a million times if only i would,
if only he could,
be with me forever, me his ghetto cinderella,
pretty girl with a' ugly limp
at first i didn't want to do it, but for he my ever true pimp,
said at worst I'd, cry my way through it

but afterwards, no words to hurt or fake,
but bread to break, a table to sup, my cup runs over
no curse, no omen, nothin' to show men,
they ain't seen already nor did
i love you momma but don't chase me no mo' and
don't come after me too, nothin you kin do,
but don't you be blue
no creed as true as that of the stroll,
old woman be glad to know,
yo' baby done grown into a' honest ho

momma's little baby love hoin', hoin'
momma's little baby love strollin' tracks
momma's little baby love strollin' strollin'
momma's little baby ain't neva' comin' back

'member when you useta, hit a' blazin' pipe torch,
to send yo shame away
t'da pie in na' sky betta day?
yet you say somebody usin' me to get pay...
freedom be between, me an them men
no curse, no omen, nothin' to show them,
they ain't seen already, nor did
the po day done hid, behind dollar signs, shine bright like,
your hot pipe light
summer night eyes an' sizzling growling belly aching away
all night awake an' holdin' you shakin, beggin you to stay but
you lef' me alone, trying to raise me now that i'm grown
my truth be da fruits you done sewn, i did my best to never
go hungry no mo
old woman you need to be knowin', your baby is well and
your baby is happy
with the daddy that got me t' hoin'
don't cha worry y'self none, it all be ova soon
we be laughin' allis away, you wit da pipe high,
me wit da sor' thigh
what tingle wit herpe venom, r'n'r, rest and laxation,

one day well gett 'em
in na pie inna' sky betta day!

me and you cain't fret where we goin',
cause the lawd knows where we been
now stand on yo feet, an' let the congregation say amen!

Twisted In My Bed

BY *Kineta James*

Tossed
bent
into 6-9 positions
spread
assumed
wide open
we had it like that
you were my man
raw as this deal we have been served,
my brother
we made revolutions
on those sheets
We have been soldiers on a Total Muscle Failure combat for
training mission, passing every obstacle
never minding the Senior Drill, his commentary or his scorecard
We soared above, dug deep and lived below the radar
2 G's in thug love
coming together for our very sanity
I have had one big knotted mangled dredlock worked into the
back of my head by the strength of your black back, and the
salty wet of your sweat

I have smelled of you for hours, even after showers
you were so into me
I exhale you
into the midnight air
where the rollers
wait for you
there, under the foggy glow
of a street lamp
the only one
conveniently staged
to illuminate
the very moment
that defined you
I keep waiting for
the hand of God to
reach into the frame
adjust the light
and the lens
so that I can see this
war for what it really is
so that my body can
take charge of my fatigues
and so my heart will
bridle her chest with courage
and so my feet
and intellectual reach can find wings
and so my tongue can
swell with truth
I did not whence
I simply prepared
and positioned my self at your back
because I am your woman
I took off the strap-on
and sent my girl home
dressed, grabbed my purse
and was on my way to see the

Bad Boys Bail Bondsman about a Black man in bondage
when the White Man in blue
told me why you were being arrested
How could you?
This union
Black Pussy - Black Dick
Is the only chance we've got of ever having a revolution
That Devil told me your sins with tears in his eyes.
How could you?
7 purposeful strikes against the womb
Assault Black Unity with poison?
7 women, you murdered with AIDS
I mean, man
You've got me twisted in my bed
7 women
I mean
8

The Master's Wife

BY *Jane Therese*

Love bows to furious rage in a curious cage called The Ghetto...
Wielded by clenched fists, Overseer's night sticks
Cocked gun...
choke hold me for a little while
As if I had not been sold to serve in the big blue house.
Alone in a concubine's suite,
there she sleeps in a casket of glass
Perfection untouched untested
Sound proof

Where is the music? Where is the music?
Confined concubine hips can not sway
In the way of ancestors
While they lay for a Master in blue
She be so beautiful so fair, he will keep her near
Like trees that fall and make no sound
When no one is around to hear
Is beauty beauty, if it is unseen?

You shattered the glass with your chains
Ran like a slave, humming prophetically
"she could never be me"
But you can't give me what I need

When all the glass had fallen, I sent my dogs to catch you
You returned battered, bruised, yet stronger for it
Together unseen, the world slumbers
I want your hands about me
But having surpassed the physical
we mystically made love mentally

Infecting me with desire to live again
Injecting danger into swollen wanton hips
Sucking venom from cursed lips
Which no longer beg for, but live of and in freedom
Why should we run away?
My blood is the putty on his walls, foundation of master's name
We should not run away.
We should run to his bed
And fuck in his bed like savages
Like savages
And watch his blue house burn in
Our afterglow

My hero
Under Master's hand
Runaway king, you, croon the song of Billy,
For I, The Master's Wife
Under Master's hand again

We should not run away.
We should run to his bed
And fuck in his bed like savages
Like savages
Like savages
And watch his blue house burn in our
afterglow

The Ghetto Unplugged

BY *Ghetto Girl Blue*

I love the taste
of your name on my lips
You are The Don
of my heart

When I lay down my pedigree
Sweet Daddy, you are right there with me
Therefore, thus and just because
I will always represent
Just like I have from the start
I still recall
Boone's Farm kisses
A delicious commitment to us
served under ghetto stars
where nature is our maitre d'
Nobody, no money, no wife, no kids, no cars,
no Hollywood gigs
could ever take that away from me
you my East Oakland Negro Hero
Spending love by the pound
My brother lover you should know
how far I'm down
to the Lower Bottoms, baby

This is your heart on trust
this is your brain on love
We are the ghetto unplugged

We are savage when we fuck
We are ridiculous
...when we make love
We don't even have to come
to know that we've arrived
Straight-up Daddykins
The Dick is live!
'Cause it's gang banging me mentally
I'm losing control of my faculty
Forgetting you're just a friend to me
Please accept my apology

Got to this place a little late
But lust like ours
can only be revealed on
CP time
Come on, sweet daddy
spill that slow wine
When our bodies intertwine
Even the moon confesses

"Ain't they fine!"

Ebonically Speaking

BY *Kineta James*

I got a hoochie secret
somethin' for you to see
Cause there ain't one thing on this earth
that feel like ghetto booty

Now I'ma flip some script to you
so you could give love to me
Sex is the ultimate conjugation
of the verb "TO BE"
It don't be just a thing we do
The way I be kissin', lickin'
and suckin' all on you
That just be an example
a display if you willin'
Can you dig it?
No pun intended
You get how I be feelin'?

I'm already knowin' cause I be seein'
the glistening snail trail
you be leavin'
And you love me so
you never fail
to drape your manhood
good and well
wit a latex condom
nice and tight
so I can give it to you right

I don't be havin' no worry
at all, when we lay safe
I am open and free
to give you this place
for your sufferin' to bury
Now I be lovin it when we fuckin'
Fuckin' is a good thing
And don't you lie
it be making you cry
to hear my pussy sing
Brother, you be conductin'
the way you be fuckin'
Arrangin' shit
Lickin' it, Slappin' it, Flippin' it,
you know how you act
like you live in it?
You can do what you want
when our Jones is on
if you knowing that this ain't gratis
The kitty be croonin'
while the music notes are tunin'
but my mind be counting C's
You's a black man with status
a brother with gees
willin' to pay pay for this fine
Gluteus Maximus

Now,
my ass cheeks be talking
when I ride your body's course
Like a stallion, poundin'
the Earth with great force
Moans, sighs, thrusts of release
I empty on that jimmy hat
all my soul vexing grief
When it be gettin' good to you
I can feel you growin' fat
Your pulse be makin'
my pussy twitch
and my legs be hella shakin'
And you be talkin' dirty
and your eyes be a wallin'
saying "Oooh baby you my bitch!"
and I don't be trippin'
hell, I love it when we ballin'
'cause ballin' is all that
Just don't you be slippin'
Tryin' to run in the cat with no hat
You best be respectin'
this body I'm protectin'
I ain't your personal love tool
I might be your "bitch"
if the cash is forthcomin'
but baby, without a rubber?
I ain't no fool!

This is for the Man in Me

BY *Kenita James*

I ain't got time for foreplay
So if you trying to play
you ain't got to stay
ain't got to lick it, just hit it
all night long

I need a raincoat without lubrication
trying to get penetration til I'm raw
Want to scream til I'm hoarse
and the neighbors call the law

This is for the man in me
I'll take it anywhere
You ain't got to hold nothin' back
just pull my fucking hair and ride it
I'll let you into any place
all fantasies are fair, don't hide it

You don't need no direction
just toss it in the air, and find it

It ain't right that it's so tight
and the pussy's calling your name like that
Now who tell me who's the mack?

Break yourself, fool
I want all the dick
And pay this chick
like the trick you are

Ghetto Superstar
that ain't what you are
You just a brotha who needs a lifejacket
If you can't swim, honey, I ain't havin it
This ain't no microwave or
no easy bake oven, this ride is over
when I say it's through
Tonight over your body I hold dominion
you can voice your opinion
when I give it to you

This is for the man in me
I'll take it anywhere
You ain't got to hold nothin' back
just pull my fucking hair and ride it
I'll let you into any place
all fantasies are fair, don't hide it

You don't need no direction
just toss it in the air, and find it

It ain't right that it's so tight
and the pussy's calling your name like that
Now who tell me who's the mack?

Set your sights for anal injection
as I swing that ass in your direction

Got you hollering like a hallelujah man
"Great Day in the mo'ning! You got good lovin'!"

If I don't see you never no mo
You'll take the memory of this ass knocking
body clocking, boot knocking, tick tocking, soul rocking
Sugar stuff to your grave

And ...

When you able to walk again,
I said, when you able to walk again
and you're on you way to hell's gate

Tell my dog Delilah I'm down here getting dicks twisted

Tell her how you got done by a real pimp up

got hosed down by the PUNANYologist

Honeycomb Hideout

BY *J Steal*

I'm not just another boy
Trying to get you behind the portables
or drag you into my Honeycomb Hideout
So I can tell my boys about how we work it out
But I'm not shy or trying to be on the down low either
If you were to
Let me
be your guy
I
Would want everybody to know.
See, ah...

I'll do anything to be your man
I'll hold your hand in public
Walk you through the projects dodging bullets
Let your friends clown me
Just to be downtown with you
Baby, even at school
I'll break all the cool rules
I'll stand in the lunch line for you,
Spend my lawn mowing money on you
I'll do anything to make this dream come true
I'll even feed you cheese fries 1   at   a   time

I'm not just another boy
Trying to get you behind the portables
or drag you into my Honeycomb Hideout
So I can tell my boys about how we work it out
But I'm not shy or trying to be on the down low either
If you were to
Let me
be your guy
I
Would want everybody to know.

I'll Spread my coat on the ground
So you can sit down

Let me kick it with you
I won't ask you to do anything you don't want to
I just want to watch your mouth move, when you talk to me
and think about your apple, Now & Later flavored lips on mine
Baby girl, I love your smile
Your teeth are so clean
They don't ever have candy stains, and them candies are
green
Come on girl, smile for me...

I've been looking for a nice girl like you
One in the smart class, One with big plans,
and everybody knows, You are up out this ghetto, soon as
you turn 18
Girl, you are like Tupac's rare rose, that grows through cracks
in concrete streets
I'm telling you these things for selfish reasons
But not the ones you're thinking...

See, I'm just a brother from the slow class,
trying to get a hall pass
to be at my locker every day, when you pass my way
See, I'm not trying to get you into my Honeycomb Hideout

When you smile...
I just want to be the thing that you are smiling about

I'm not just another boy
Trying to get you behind the portables
or drag you into my Honeycomb Hideout
So I can tell my boys about how we work it out
But I'm not shy or trying to be on the down low either
If you were to
Let me be your guy
I would want everybody to know.

Sisters in Xstacy

BY *Ghetto Girl Blue*

I'm not a religious woman,
but I know how to love my sister

Don't want you to have to go to Jesus
Want you to build an altar on my soul and
Lay your burdens down
My sister in xstacy

With sister fellowship I will help bear your cross
With a little help from our sisters

I'm not a religious woman
My mouth is too full of soul healing tales to chant
Nam myoho renge kyo
Into the mirrored belly of Buddha

For, when I see your face
Distorted with pain...
I have seen my reflection!

When I nurse the wounds your lover leaves
Across your heart,
Your body, your Face,
I have healed my own wounds

And when you cry alone at night
Thinking no one hears
believing Man's God
Has turned a deaf ear to the Sisters

I am hoarse in the morning
too hoarse, my sister, to wait for God

I wail for you,
I wail for you, my sister
and our unified voices
send those demons straight back
to hell for you, my sister
to hell for you, my sister

Lady's Room

BY *Jessica Holter*

Towels for tips.
It was a modest existence,
but entertaining,
to say the very least.

Club life releases the beast...
Carnality.

The Lady's Room
was more like a lion's den.
A cage for malevolence,
cattiness
to masquerade itself
in heavy perfume
designer costume
flawless coif
intricately designed claws
that could effortlessly remove
prowling jealous eyes from their sockets
stealing confidence from competitors like pick-pockets

They came here to stand in my mirror
pretending to powder their noses,
Out tipping. Striking poses.
Eliminating opposition.
Loudly divulging secrets across stalls
I sold tampons, lip gloss, weed, roses,
mints, gum, and condoms in lockets,
clocking duckets in buckets
pretending not to really be there
and not to care, but cleaning the floor
as the least of them fall on to it

covetous greed
painfully desirous
competition
to win the affinity
of the lionized male
who hunts for felines
who dare go toe to toe to win
a night of sublime good times

Cat fights are bloody
creating wounds that cut deep into the soul
where the heart pumps worthiness
a measurable source of a temporary life
that is defeated by the union of
Mother Nature and Father Time
whose hands are mighty,
not to be placated by vanity

They followed her into my office
A pride of lions
boasting, primping, preying
eliminating

She could have been any one of them,
frolicking about this diamond-studded jungle
where the meek die in the dust
She was just a cub. Nervous.
A little girl in The Lady's Room of a club
unprepared for this warfare,
that was but a primal circus of lust.

I found her sobbing and vomiting
into the toilet
squatting before it
in the stall reserved for the handicapped
She couldn't understand how I knew
that she was pregnant
but confessed it
through tears of regret

I put the "out of order" sign on
The Lady's Room door
Consoled her in discourse
preparing her for this course
a testament, I said, to the wonderment
of motherhood,
a gift for which
catty pussy holds no merit
Wiping her tears away,
convincing her that she could bear it
I picked her up off the floor
and sent her home
to prepare for her war

It was a modest existence.
Towels for tips.

But every once in a while
I gave them more.

The Cutting
of the Rose

BY *Ghetto Girl Blue*

Though you talk to me with sweetness
on your breath and in your heart,
My body will not rise to feel
your meaning in whole, or in part.

I am a woman without a doubt
my servitude is the measure,
Your expectant stance and countenance
is but my single pleasure.

You will never have to worry, my love
If I shall ever stray,
For the offending thorn of my desire
has been sharply cut away.

Tuned and pruned to suit my groom
I am the comely bride,
Submitting to my husband's will
without desire but with pride.

I am free from worldly sins
for the path I chose,
May Allah bless the garden keepers
for the cutting of the rose.

What is female circumcision?

Female circumcision, also called female genital **mutilation**, involves removing part of a female's external genitalia (reproductive organs). It is a **cultural practice** that began about 2,000 years ago in Africa. Female circumcision continues to be practiced by some tribal African cultures, as well as by some Middle Eastern and Indonesian cultures.

Among the reasons for the procedure are to ensure that a female is a virgin when she gets married and to **reduce** the female's ability to experience **sexual pleasure**, which decreases the chance of extra-marital affairs.

Sunna circumcision — This involves the removal of the tip of the clitoris and/or its hood or covering (prepuce).

Clitorectomy — This is the removal of the entire clitoris and the adjacent labia (the external and internal folds of skin, or lips, that protect the vaginal opening).

Infibulation — This procedure involves performing a clitorectomy, including the removal of the labia. The tissues are then sewn together, leaving only a small hole for the flow of urine and menstrual blood. In many cases, a second procedure is necessary later to allow for sexual intercourse.

Confessions of a Lipstick Lesbian

BY *Jessica Holter*

I fucked a man for twelve years, and the only stick that could make me cum ... came with AA batteries in a brown paper bag from a little pink boutique that squatted on a dismal Oakland street. I hid the clear plastic drill, complete with a rotating head and spinning pearls from my man, beneath the underwear in a drawer beside the bed we shared. My "Friend," as I liked to call the thing. would comfort me in the morning after I had suffered through a long night of cumlessness, feeling my lips swell with pain and want between my legs.

My man never seemed to notice, or care for that matter if I had experienced a pleasure similar to his. He seemed to believe, in his arrogance, that I derived some euphoric ecstasy from tasting the bitter nut of him spill over my lips onto my tongue. He believed it. So I believed it. I thought my pleasure was in seeing him pleased. I knew no balance.

That is, until Jewel.

Jewel was not the type of girl any man was attracted to beyond a romp between sheets, if she was ever lucky enough to be offered the comfort of his bed. More often than not, she serviced them like luxury cars through detail shops in backseats, hotel bathrooms, elevators, the alleyway that stretched behind the exotic dance club in which she teased them. Before services were rendered she was ... well paid.

We sat Indian style, facing each other on a mohair rug in the middle of her living room in an Emeryville high-rise as I tried to concentrate on the words rather than on the lightly glossed pouting lips that spoke them. The most horrid of stories laced through the silk of her sultry voice inviting me to lick her wounds clean, soften her hardened heart with a tender female hand.

I only fuck men for money, she said delicately, placing an electrifying hand on my knee that sent shock waves through me. But, she said, she did not consider herself any more of a whore than the wife of a Wall Street banker she boned in the bathroom of an airplane once.

Jewel gave me pleasure I had never known before that day. In her embrace I found peace and as her tongue penetrated my essence, tears flowed into my ears muffling my cries of passion and her moans of hunger. Rivers of ecstasy oozed, filling her, parching me. With wet sloppy kisses she moistened my mouth. I smelled my womanhood on her breath, her lips, and on the caramel skin of her face. In that solitary moment I understood the unrelenting thirst for pussy. I wondered longingly, silently, as my mouth and fingers scrambled to her core, if she would taste as luscious on my lips as I had tasted on my own.

I do not know where Jewel is today. Maybe married, maybe dead, maybe both. She confessed she would marry a man someday, have babies, cook dinners, die slowly...

As for me, give me pussy or give me death.

Masturbation

Masturbation is not only a **safe** alternative to sexual intercourse, it is also a great opportunity to get to know the **magic of your own body.** With the assistance of your own hands, sterilized toys, and your **creative** imagination, your **body** can take you to **places** the unskilled partner can not even dream of. **But be careful!** Some toys can be so **powerful,** masturbation can quickly become an **addiction,** or a preference for achieving orgasm. (I have yet to meet a penis or a tongue that can emulate the strength and precision of "The Rabbit" or the "Hitachi Magic Wand"!) Mutual **Masturbation** is another great alternative to intercourse. In this **self-stimulating** scenario, live **visual** stimuli of another person sharing the experience with you, adds the **human touch** that machines can not duplicate. But beware, sharing toys is not advised so **BYOT.** — Ghetto Girl Blue

A PSA from **A.F.A.C.T.**
Artists Fighting AIDS Creatively Through the Arts.

Boi, Let me Lick Your Pussy

BY *T. Calloway*

If we are cursed
to Hell with me,
Boi, let me lick your pussy

Butterfly, open wide
Let your scent fill all of my
senses with promises
that only your
sweet   black   pussy
can make good on

I don't want a daddie,
boi, not tonight
Just let me lick your pussy

Let my tongue trail
the walls of your
upper
inner
thighs
receive me like the woman
you were born to be
not the man you want to be

Take off the strap
I want the sap
Girl, let me lick your pussy

Let your body heat call to me
open up your well
climb on my face
and
sit
a spell

Pretend you are me, if you must
trust me when I say
There is an art to being on top
and there's an art to getting fucked

No pillow princess, am I tonight, sweetie
Let me lick your pussy

Tear down your walls, baby
Those are lips, not balls
So, come on, Boi
and kiss me

High Is My Dream

BY *T. Calloway*

I awaken in a purple haze.
A maze of infinite possibilities,
sleepwalking in a place
that defies space and time.

Pinch me lover.

I could have been anyone, someone great
Gone anywhere, some place grand!
But no matter the path I took,

I look back
and find a gravitational pull
that leads always back to you.

Like Lot's wife,
I became
as salt,
good only for seasoning
your tongue

Brown Girl

BY *T. Calloway*

brown girl laughs through walls
promises ot betrayal
pushing closed my doors

One Stroke at a Time

BY *Kineta James*

Across a ghetto room; not a room really, more like an old garage, not safe enough for cars, yet they assembled there;

To find a ghetto blue promise of love; after systematic death, that ghetto life brought; He saw her

That Jack leg DJ spun them records for 2 bottles of Irish Rose and a bottle of Boone's Farm; rocking that place till minds spun as fast as that vinyl;

With promises of the good life; not the good life really, more like a day, a moment, a millisecond of freedom;

That's when he saw her dancing; not dancing really, more like spinning by; getting his head all twisted up in her wraparound skirt and two hints of the thighs underneath;

Her body burned with proof that Satin was a fallen angel from heaven; beautiful to behold; but the haze of the smokey dim lit not exactly a room kind of place, played tricks on his eyes.

Outside it was quite dark and very quiet; very dark; but not quite so quiet enough that he could not hear the crack in her voice;

By the time he figured out the truth about this chick; not a chick really since she had a dick; that those creamy thighs, spinning ass, and sucking plans were really whispered on the sweet breath of a man;

He had a foot-long hard-on stroking knee deep thinking fuck it; it ain't a woman but the bitch is fine, suicide one stroke at a time.

Switch

BY *Kenita James*

I sing to thee of Switch
A player who never kept it real
Pressed and dressed
he looked his best
for each lady he served with his thrill

Now he wasn't called Switch
for the blade he carried
and all the busters he put in a ditch
It was for the sweet love he gave
in ghetto serenade
the name followed him from days
when he was a prison bitch

Between prison walls
Taboo passion falls
And Switch licked dicks and balls
With the skill of Vanessa Del Rio

Now the ladies
could never really know
or recognize the real lies
hidden behind his night eyes

the sudden twist of his style
the creeping smirk in his smile
or the dual tone of his moans
they came in droves
'cause he sucked toes
and left no fantasy stones
unturned

By the time they learned
of his prison bitch days
they faced death's gaze
laying up with AIDS
their mommas mourning bedside
plotting their graves

The War Between Tops & Bottoms

BY *T. Calloway*

Late.
her hips pressed
against my ass

Hot.
because he was watching

It's like that?

It could be.
but what she
really wants to do
is fuck a man in the ass

Like that?
Yep.
She's never done it before. I lied, not knowing it yet.
Forty-five minutes and a bridge ride later
my phone rang...

"Booty Call,
        Booty Call,
                Booty Call!"

I wondered if I could download that ring
and set it for the men
who phone disrespectfully
after 10 o'clock pm

It was 2:15 in the morning
"Is it cool?
I'm on my way to your pad."
I looked at my woman
as if to ask permission
She returned a sly glance as if to say,
"Bring it on!"
Five minutes inside
he was just parking
but she was already
showered and strapped

I had seen her that way many times
her plump ass squeezed between 3 black leather straps
holding in place a 9-inch dick
I had handpicked from Good Vibrations
to match the John Henry hunk of the man
I used to call my husband
It was large, slightly flexible, jet black
and bulged with human vein-like texture
I had a special relationship to this dick
It was mine
and I was particular about it.
to me, it was as real as any dick,
as in relationships
it would only stray if I got careless and lost it
or as in tonight, chose to give it away.

It was huge next to her small body
but trust,
she wore it and used it like she had grown it
She was soft butch, bisexual by admission
and beautiful by even Hollywood standards
If she were an ice cream she'd be a Creole Mocha Blend
A tiny package, she was, full of surprises
Hairs on her chin
Egotistical and a Taurus
even her cum smelled like a man's
Yet her breasts were nearly as large as mine
and I was busting provocatively out of a double D

I'd lie if I said living this life
didn't bring thoughts of
Jerry Springer to my mind from time to time
I giggled like the child I felt like
anticipating
Nowhere to hide

She made a cup of coffee.
sipped it wearing nothing
but the dick and strap
I blushed.
abandoned her to the shower
doorbell rings
I scrubbed and tried to wash off the vodka
so I could know that this was really happening
Now let me get this straight...
rinsing my cigarette breath again
spitting water
My former lover
Is coming over
to let my lesbian lover
fuck him in the ass
I shook my head a couple times
but the thought was still there

My heart would not stop racing
it wasn't sexual excitement
I was pretty sure of that

It felt more like the nerves that flutter about your stomach
when you know you have done wrong and your momma has
found out
but you haven't made it home yet
and your sister is running toward you
shouting
ooooh, you gonna get it!
Accepting the inevitable
you can only hope she falls.

I had known him for as long as I had known my own sexual
being
I was a virgin when we met
He introduced me to the freak in me
and has kept her skills on point for nearly 20 years
but never this way
Damn!

My momma told me he was gay!
I was thinking this, when he stepped into the shower
He washed my body
kissed me everywhere
just like he used to
and did that thing he does with his thumbs
massaging my inner thighs down to the bone
gently stretching my pussy with circular motions
until I had the urge to press down
and give birth to another level of
our homie-lover-friendship
I was melting in the heat
I cooled the water down
Kissed the softest lips I have ever known
and said goodbye to love making as I had known it with him

My momma
and the women of her generation
would have stopped us dead in our tracks
because there are some things you just don't hang out to dry
What was going down tonight
was definitely going to leave some dirty laundry

She made it easy to get started
She didn't believe in awkward moments
He stepped out of the shower
She pushed me into him
He held me tight
lit a joint, passed it around
The kissing commenced quickly
I couldn't suck her pussy with the strap on
and her legs so tight, like they always are for me
so I sucked her dick
then his
He ate my pussy
then tongue kissed her ass
She ate my pussy then tongue kissed him
then put her tongue to his rim
for a very long time

he wanted to enter her
she wasn't having it
I stepped out of the room to grab two rubbers
while they decided who's on top
and what's on second
I don't know,
third base came so quickly
I didn't have time to think

I sat back and took a lesson in testosterone
waiting just a few moments to see if
he would give the ass up right away

A few more of her famous tongue lashings
inside and outside of his ass hole
she was going to be in there
I couldn't bare to watch him go out like that
I wanted to know, but I couldn't watch

So I did what any woman
in denial about the sexual preference
of a man she's loved since childhood would do...
I slipped my body under his
shoving hips into his
I spread my legs
Spread them wide
opened my pussy up in the candlelight
Wet my finger
slapped my clit
pushed two fingers in and out of my self
testing the waters with my own tongue
and
attempted to flood the room
with the intoxicating pheromones
of my good pussy
but all I could smell was ass
as she dug into him
with such aggression,
her force urged him deeper inside of me.

Part of me hoped for a fast win in this
war between tops and bottoms
for the sake of my health
Cuz this was 2004
and I had been fucking a man who
desired a dick in his ass
for nearly half of my life

The other parts of me were
extremely turned on
extremely jealous
and angry
over how I had been a sexual fool
seeing all the signs, heeding no warning
What was more, I hadn't even been giving him,
what he was really looking for

My body grew hotter
as he kissed me and briefly remembered me
calling my name
I drew my pussy like an M16
and fired into the dark
He spread my thighs wider
Fucked me with his tongue
Sucking my fat pussy lips
on the up stroke
a couple feet away could hear her tongue
lathering up his ass
His hips began to roll
Pow she slapped it with a magical sting
and raised the ass high into the air
with the power possessed in her fingertips

My man was now my woman's bitch
And the 9-inch dick I had picked
from a little Berkeley sex boutique,
that reminded me of my husband,
and gave to my lesbian lover
to fuck me with,
was in my soulmate's ass
deeply, in his ass
"Stop."
he pronounced
candy in my ears

She withdrew

He caught his breath
Then whispered
"Tell her to put it back in."
My pussy got numb.

He continued to fuck me, I think.
Mostly, she fucked him
She fucked him, and busted so many times
before they finally came together
Their unified moans and grunts
were like a song, a dirty rap song
I added some curse words and moans
of my own but my pussy was only wet
with her juices
as they shot on his ass and thighs
and drip down to tease me.

But he still wanted to enter her
in four years, I hadn't even put a finger inside of her
she almost didn't lay down for that
gave it the political lesbian try
before her legs were spread so far apart
I didn't recognize her or her porn star vocabulary

The pair weren't fighting anymore
"Thank you, thank you, thank you"
he repeated emphatically
over and over as he dressed

He really meant that shit.
I had two G's in my bed
giving me the kind of truth
you don't even get in church

I had no reason to be mad
I set the whole thing up
I had asked for a pass to a game that was not for suckers
He wanted something that I wasn't willing to give
and now that I know this
I can choose not to put myself at risk

I wasn't mad anymore.
because I was no longer a fool,
just maybe a little grossed out.
I mean, accept for the fact that
the entire room smelled like ass
It might have even been cool.

But the thought of where his ass goes
on nights he can't find a woman
so willing to engage in anal play
was a little bit scary

It was 4:15 he went home to his wife
I drank my girl's cold coffee
Sat down at my computer and ordered
a new dick online

Home Testing

If you get a **positive** HIV test that is not anonymous, or if you get any medical services for HIV infection your **name** will be reported to the Department of Health.

But... **Don't** let embarrassment or conspiracy theory be the reason you may be **exposing others** to HIV/AIDS. You can now **test yourself** for HIV/AIDS in the **privacy** of your own home.

There are home tests for sale online.

For more information visit www.TestYourselfAtHome.com

or type "at home, AIDS, Test" in your favorite search engine

If you become **infected** with HIV, it usually takes between three weeks and two months for your **immune system** to produce antibodies to HIV. If you think you were exposed to HIV, you should **wait for two months** before being tested.

For more information about HIV/AIDS visit www.AIDS.org.

Hood Wife

BY *Jessica Holter*

Seritha wondered how much further she could spread her legs apart. She wondered how much deeper Donny could enter her body. She wondered how much more of herself she would have to give, before he would recognize her devotion to him and give her the respect she deserved.

She had, after all, been his hood wife for more than three years, shamelessly answering his every sexual desire with the lust that burned within her like an inferno. Hadn't she aborted two babies at his insistence? Hadn't she kept their relationship a secret hidden in the lower bottoms of Oakland, far from China Hill where he lived a clean life with his clean wife and perfect little mixed children?

She had told herself that it would end soon if he did not commit soon, but soon could not come soon enough. For, every time she saw him, every time she heard his voice, every time she even thought of him, she would become, as an obedient child.

Earlier tonight, sitting on her porch, waiting for him to come, she vowed this would be the last time. But when he arrived, her heart turned to putty. And when Jackie, the only girl in the neighborhood pretty enough to be considered her rival, watched with envy as she stepped to the big black sedan, Seritha's ego took over and nothing she had promised herself mattered.

She rode in silence, gazing at the full moon as it followed them to a remote parking space near a gentle brook on the UC Berkeley Campus that navigated its course with the erotic resonance that only wetness can evolve to.

Now the moon was immobile, hanging in the night like a giant stage prop watching her as she lay, face down, on the hood of his Mercedes, the running engine warming her skin. She was a seasoned lover now, knowing what to do and say at all the right times to please him. It didn't matter to her that she never came. Giving into him had always pleased her.

"Seritha, you are not wet."

"I'm sorry."

"Don't be sorry, baby. Relax."

"I'm trying to." Donny did not speak another word. He grabbed her ankles, and spread them so far apart her pussy caught the night's chill. He immersed his tongue deep inside of her pressing his nose into her ass hole. It might have been the very thing she needed but it hurt her legs, and she didn't know how to tell him. He worked his tongue around for a few minutes, but in this position she could not grind against his face to entice her fluids to come down.

"What's wrong with you, girl? You don't taste like anything." He violently crossed her ankles and flipped her over. Her back and head slammed into the hood of the car. She hadn't noticed the song of the midnight birds until they were frightened away by the sound. "I'm sorry, baby, did that hurt?" It did, but Seritha said that it didn't."I wasn't talking to you I was talking to my car," he said laughing. "Just kidding. Now tell me the truth, lady. You haven't been douching, have you?"

"No, why would I do that?"

Donny looked suspiciously at her, but seemed to accept her answer.

He pulled her down the hood of the car so that her thighs rested against his cheeks, and kissed her pussy, first with his lips and then with his tongue. He made tiny circular motions on her clit, pausing occasionally to see if she had become aroused. But she remained dry.

Donny was becoming angry. He stood, towering over her, looking down on her. The moon seemed to shrink into a sad little face over his left shoulder.

He was more than six feet tall. She had mastered the terrain of his body years ago, but now he seemed like a stranger to her. Out of his suit, standing there in his wife beater, his Calvin Klein underwear pulled down around his bowed thighs, he looked like any niggah from the hood. The shaft she had come to adore was threatening. In his anger, even his dialect regressed.

"Spit on it," he commanded.

Seritha hesitated but did as she was told. She sat up, wrapped her hand around his dick and licked its head.

Donny grabbed her hair, and cocked her head, so that he could see her face; so that she could see him speaking to her.

"Did I say lick it?" He forced her head left and right. "No, I didn't, did I? I said spit on it!"

Seritha sucked spit from her glands, rolled it in her tongue and spit on Donny's dick.

"That's it.Again!"

Seritha spit again.

Donny's dick got harder, his veins pulsated against his shaft. He pushed her down on the car, still holding her hair in one hand, his dick in the other, and shoved himself into her dry, tight pussy. Seritha screamed in pain. But Donny thrust deeper into her. She screamed again, and again he thrust inside her. The more she screamed, the more he loved it.

Seritha didn't mean to cry but she couldn't dam her tears. And once she started crying she couldn't stop

Donny slowed his pace but didn't stop fucking Seritha.

"Awe girl, don't start that shit again. I know you're not punking up on me," he said, letting go of her hair and wiping her tears. Seritha reached for this moment of tenderness, wanting desperately to hold on to it. His eyes softened and his lip curled, in that familiar naughty way that it had when he first met her at the beauty supply store, where she worked. He had been so squared off then, in classic Stacy Adams, a herring-bone suit and a one-inch Afro in desperate need of hair sheen. He came for human hair for his wife, and left with make-over tips and an invitation to her place to get a texturizer.

"Seritha, you hear me talking to you?"

"Huh?" she asked, choking back tears.

Donny rubbed his thumb across her lips. "I asked if you are a cry baby? Because if you are, I thought you might want to suck my thumb." Seritha opened her mouth to speak and Donny shoved his thumb in her mouth, pumping furiously inside of her. He pulled his thumb from her mouth, reached under her and shoved it in her ass.

Seritha turned her face away from Donny, and let him have his way with her, in the night, near the brook, under the shrinking moon, and let the tears flow.

Baby Dolls

BY *Kineta James*

For Baby Dolls it all begins with a glance
Across your face, your well-suited stance
She's mesmerized by the way you dance
Hypnotized in a sexual fantasy trance
Could this be her last chance?
For emancipation?
Soul elation?
District Attorney administration?
Her imagination
hangs on your pants.

It's evident she's perking a bit
and her eyes say she wants to do you.
As she walks to you,
clad in midnight blue
Dress spread so tight 'round well-placed pounds
It looks like her thighs are having a fight
and her mounds are egging them on
A promising sight...

She says she thought she knew you
From a dream she had last night
And that in it you were hungry
And she soothed your appetite.
But just in case you're just diggin the scene
And not trying to remember how
I tossed it up in your dreams
I could refresh your memory if you'd give me a call,
The number is 555-6969
Make the time to take my dime
And a quarter and I'll be glad to take your order.
I'll be kickin it at the club till 2
But I'm makin' breakfast when this is through.
Don't you sleep on the late night creep
'Cause I may have to serve my own plate
I'm in the Lakeside Plaza don't be too late
Buzz for Donna Ball at the gate.

Damn you're thinking,
Wouldn't it be nice to be freaking?
But she looks like she just came from the mall
Just another baby doll,
With sugar walls, paging late night for booty calls.

But you've got two babies' mommas
Taxing your check before you get it
You ain't trying to regret it
Because the kids are sweet but you bet it
Would have been different
If you weren't so quick to get
It on with every Baby Doll you met
Let it be known that it's cheaper to keep her
Who was that who said it?
All them baby dolls with sugar walls
Paging late night for booty calls

And though your eyes watch
The jiggling as it's wiggling away
Your conscience is rambling about family and having the
Patience to wait for a good one

And the balls it takes to stay
Telling you, Baby Dolls are luxury toys
Just DA ploys to keep you from a new life
Your wits are sharp as a Ginsu knife
Don't need no more strife and you can tell
By Donna's weave, her outfit, and her nails
The molestation of your financial situation
Would not make this one your wife.

So you sit down and look around
Just then you see her...
She's simple and plain
Her hair is short, it's natural and it's tame
And you're drawn to her corner of the cabaret
By the faintest scent of spring rain
She's writing poetry in a notebook
Called my heart's last pain
When you step to her and say

"Yo, while you're writing, baby doll,
Jot down your number and your name."

But she closes the book and says
I'm not your baby doll with sugar walls
Paging late night for booty calls
If you want to know my name,
it's plain and simply Jane
And I need a man who's simply the same

Not the average man with late breakfast plans
But one who can find the book of my mind
Open it, and know how to read it
Are you even literate?

Think you could liberate my spirit
Then show me how you freed it?
Could you recognize that my life
Is my own, yet yours to share?
Lend a hand to make we a pair
Or would you take control and try to lead it?

Can you take a deadened heart
And show me I still need it
Or unfold my brain to mysteries untold
And ever gently seed it?

Sure you could flower my womb
Till I'm dead in my tomb
Catching me at full bloom
Before the 28th day of each month
But could you pollinate my soul
Never trying to penetrate my whole
I'm a sista who knows
Enfamil and baby clothes
Is no fair trade to keep a man on file

The late night creep is infantile
To make my body smile
He need only kiss my mind
He being my teacher,
my friend, love artist
provision soldier
Down to ride till the battle is over

I'm not desperate or blind
I can see who you are
and no pager-friendly nightclub star
Could ever get far
with sistas who know who they are.

You feel your back bow
under the pressure
Of the truth she told
Slap your conscience once
then twice for extra measure

Gesture for the waitress
to fetch you another Fetzer.
Then ego steps in, that old captain save a bro
He's like, "G, you can't be alone!"
You might go home
and find her poetry singeing your soul,
And befall some change of heart.

So you walk away tall,
feeling your eyes scan the wall
For a hint of that chick Donna Ball
Cause you've discovered that after all,

You need a Baby Doll
with sugar walls
Paging late night
for booty calls

Deeper than Death

FOR THE SOLDIERS

BY *Ghetto Girl Blue*

The moon changed thrice tonight
and we are at war.

The Matrix.

Even the beat of my heart
is but an allusion

My eyes cry
Napalm dust.

The man in the box
tallies numbers
but only the mothers of the dead remember
the names of the first to swallow death
in enemy sands,
where home is but a mirage
baring the reflection

of his lover's hips

his momma's meals

his homeboys...
battalions of boys
fighting manhood

Lord, do I prepare my table in vain?

Send my soldier home
with everything in its place

So that he may eat.

So that I might nourish him
and bring him
back to life again

Pretty and ſmart

BY *DJ Blackmon*

It seems from the surface
That my appearance makes a claim
That my head is full of air
But I bear the burden of the blame

You see, "Pretty is as Pretty does"
Is something people say just because
They assume that if I'm attractive
There's no reason for my mind to be active

But that couldn't be further from fact
You see, that brainless role is just an act
It plays on egos, sympathies, and matters of the heart
Because fools believe that stereotype,
that Pretty can't be Smart.

I let them believe it and play the role
Cause Pretty gives me access, and Smart gives me control
Pretty frees me from responsibility,
they assume that I don't know
Smart tells me to keep quiet not to let my knowledge show

Batting my lashes while my winning smile flashes
My curves speaking body languages,
invoking images of splashes
Pretty weaves a magic so that Smart things can begin
Cause Smart knows Pretty works on more than just men.

So when they assume I'm not intelligent I don't defend
I just feign being wounded and continue to pretend
I know my power is in the illusion that I'm an air head at heart
But the truth be told the cards I hold are Pretty and Smart

The Perfect Pussy

BY *J Steal*

All of the warning signs were there.
No Hunting.
Many had been in this place before me,
facing the beast
Teetering between the thirst for Her
And the thirst to destroy Her

Cage her wild freedom
With love and obsession
The box forbids transgression
Douse the fire in her eyes
Pluck the pheromone
from her flesh
and yes,
Baptize her insatiable desires

A crusade for equality!
A fast kill!
To the hunting grounds again!

There She was,
Flawless butterscotch skin.
Feline stride.
Two green cat eyes,
Hidden from daylight,
Behind the shade of her brim.

I was a lone traveler
Cruising the cape of a motherland
Shamelessly raped and reborn
Of its ancestors blood,
And its perpetrator's hunting will.

Her awesome presence
Caught my breath
Put a choke hold on my heart…

I mean
I've had
A bank teller
A choir director
A waitress and a cook
Writing me checks
Singing my praise
Serving my needs
And feeding my greed

I have had 25 kills
In as many days
But I
I could not draw my weapon.

Let me get to the point.
I've had a Ph.D. on my MIC
A lawyer with bountiful connections
A preacher's wife in full confession
And a businesswoman-turn-chamber-maid
In my bed of deception
A gymnast, with 4 double joints

We brought
19 positions to perfection
A kindergarten teacher with more heart than Vanessa
Del Rio could not go to the depths of her lesson
I mean

I have had 25 kills, in as many days
But I... I could not draw my weapon.

There they were.
Spread my shoulder's width apart
Two streams of flesh-tone silk
Running endlessly into
A pair of black patent leather pumps
With just enough heel to be
deemed "naughty"

They said she was uppity, ornory, haughty
But they might as well
have been speaking French
that day and hence,
For all I heard was the throbbing pulse
That thumped against
the walls of her lightly scented neck

Anais, Anais
Release me

For all of my captures
I could not escape the rapture
Of the perfect pussy
Tucked neatly between
Two thunderous thighs
That promised
A mother's love
A whore's loyalty
There was only one rule.

"Never hit it twice."

How to Have an Orgasm for $500

BY *Jessica Holter*

she was always kind of euphoric
dreamy and deep thinking
and spontaneous
and emotional
and very difficult to satisfy sexually
in the days before her cycle began,
but nothing could have prepared her for that night.

she watched him sleeping,
in awe, dumb struck - struck dumb, for the moment
as his stress-filled face was blanketed in angelic rebirth,
resting for a time
every wrinkle, settled snuggly in its own place
telling its own tale of
worry, sadness, laughter
the search was over
relaxed, flawed and perfect
she knew right then that she loved him
wanted him beyond any boundary
but there were always so many

and though she carried the weight of the world on her stiletto
pumps through the east coast fall
she danced in the blessing of a moment in time
that offered a rare gift
he wanted nothing but the presence of her while in his solitude

she watched as his eyes darted beneath the shield of their lids
in search of a long awaited dream.

she kissed her tiny manicured fingertips and pressed them on
his eyes

they seemed to flutter with an awareness of her,
that made her feel
well, a bit fuzzy inside
(with all of her worries she had not known the feeling
in some time.)

he continued to search for dreams
she wanted to talk to him
but dared not upset the moment

it was cold outside that night
and she was hot with insatiable flames that she alone could not
seem to keep at bay.

she embodied her own heat in a scarlet raw silk dress that
clasped her body like a frightened pussy cat. i mean tight...
"thelma evans" tight.
she adored red. the color made her feel mischievous… "black
shampoo" mischievous.

9 ? weeks in a night naughty.

it was october, the hunt was on
and she had been watching videos for far too long

she stepped out of the door, walked down 15th street to the
corner of l

washington, d.c. prostitutes were a sight to see on friday night
they took the pavement under their feet like a runway
worked it.
waving, bending, fluttering exaggerated lashes
donned from mane to toe in glamour

diplomats, denoted by their license plates directed drivers
to circle, to circle, to circle

round firm asses
round firm breasts
big, bold hair

around and around like a merry go
so much to behold she was dizzy
watching them always made her dizzy, wanton

she didn't know how long she had been watching
she just stood there in a trance
throbbing

sequins and satin glaring through headlights.

the blast of a horn honking snapped her to
just in time to feel her purse snatched from her hand

just enough time
to watch it run away

"she's around here every night, this time, you know."

her eyes followed the voice, miles above a streaming,
seamless cobalt-blue mystical being that seemed to speak with
an echo

"just hold up here tomorrow night, and she'll probably try to sell
it back to you. then you can commence to whipping her little
crackhead ass!"

she just stood there. watching the light shine bright green, like
a halo around this 6-foot-4-inch transsexual goddess.

"light's green, honey. light's green," the goddess said, grabbing her arm and guiding her across the street, into the post pub tavern, to a table in the back, where they were sitting together when she came to.

"whiskey, honey. i don't need to ask if you need a drink, i got you a whiskey. drink it. you are just a little shell shocked. since i haven't seen you around here before, i'm guessing it's your first night."

"my first night?" she asked when she finally spoke. she took the whiskey shot and asked for another.

they sat forever.
the goddess talking about the magic of her life, jewels, travels, tricks, treats, successes, defeats

listening, learning.

"you're a hot girl, huh? honey, hot isn't good in this game. in this game there are only two kinds of women that make it: the ones who understand what men want and the ones who are men."

"are you looking to get laid or get paid?"

"never, never, never, expect an orgasm from a client. the climax comes at the mall! i swear it." the goddess laughed that beautiful echoing song as she stood to put her head back in the clouds.

and, leaving, said,

"i swear it, Miss Lady, one day you'll be standing in the shoe department at macy's: evan picone pumps to your left, gucci purses to your right, and in the distance … a full-length winter white wonder of a leather trench coat and her cousins, eggshell and taupe, all pining for your attention. a full set of louis vuitton travel gear, a trip to paris for you and your muva on your mind, and the money in your pocketbook to pay for it all and splash! right there in the middle of the mall!

the goddess was gone when he walked in.
his face contorted with stress

she didn't think about it.

she just walked over and sat down next to him
ordered whatever he was having and filled him with an open ear

he was an editor at the newspaper across the street
he nearly missed a deadline
the story was about a friend and co-worker
sued for sexual harassment
on the cusp of the anita hill scandal

"well you know" she said, reading the fading words on his pro
marion barry sweatshirt,
"that bitch set barry up."

it had only taken 30 seconds for her to like him
30 minutes to break his tension
and 15 more to be in the hotel room he kept on reserve for
nights like these

she sucked the remains of any stress from his staff

now he lay there
in the slim light of the cars outside, seeping through the partial-
ly drawn curtains
ever searching
for someone to share a moment like this magical one

she really hated to disturb him.

really.

but he had fallen to sleep before she could get undressed, let
alone, cum.

her heart raced as she kissed his eyelids to wake him.

"baby, i have to go now. are you alright?"

he smiled this biggest brightest smile.

"girl, you took a year off my life."

"i don't know if that's good or bad."

"that's definitely good.
when can I see you again?"

"i'm glad. tomorrow, after I come from the mall."

"i see. How much do you need?"

"$500."

"a steal," he said.

she could feel the orgasm
building, all the way home.

if she saw the crackhead on the way home
she just might
buy her own purse back
just
for that sake of the game.

Player's Ball

This is Verbal Penetration
An erotic conversation
Something like mental masturbation
I'm diggin' this sensation
Sex, Theater & Education
Flows of another persuasion
black, white, red or Asian
Punany is not lost in translation
Cuz the players ball, yeah the players
You know the players ball
Grab a rubber make a booty call
From folks in Oakland to Australians
Punany's feeling your frustration
What's up with bug chasin'?
This is a baller's coronation
A safer sex demonstration
That doesn't appeal to degradation
Punany gives new meaning to liquidation
Just try to keep your concentration
Cuz the players ball, yeah the players
You know the players ball
Grab a rubber make a booty call

Watch the ass drop, Poetic beats knock
Mind fucking you so deep, you get brain lock
Cuz we keep it hot for the first black sexual revolution
HBO, London 5, keeping it live, Cinemax
Don't PlayBoy - I got Lex in the City on my titty
and I'm birthin' poetic babies
on BET, even my molesting daddy
can't fade me like that
I'm GGB,
this is my Life Track

Hey Pahtna

BY *Jockey G*

I jis got me a paper about AIDS slipped to me by my homie and I wants to apply for some. Could I get an application? You got to mail it to my momma house though, cause I don't want my girl knowin how much I'm gettin. I'm on disability, on a count of I got dis ability to sleep all day. I been getting all kinds of AIDS from the govment cause my babies mommas be participatin in all the programs yall be offerin. Now it look like I can get AIDS for sex.

Its a damn shame that this here AIDS for Sex comes so late because I'm known as Jock in da street cause all the hoes I ride. What I really want to know is, Can I get back pay for all the sex I already had? I read that the mo sex I have, the mo chance I got of gettin AIDS. Somebody owe a fool.

I wants to thank yall fo' letting me know dat using condoms can stop me from gettin AIDS, cause I got this new female that be buggin'. But I'ma let yall know I still qualify for AIDS because latex don't come tween Jock and sex. Haah, I'm a poet, bet yall didnt know it!

Anyway, I been xsplainin to my women that the govment gon be payin us for all the sex we have. Man I be heck of tired cause all my women startin to see we cant let no kind a AIDS slip by.

Da other day I was thankin bout settlin down with my old lady Quanisha, but I was readin' that the mo sex partners I have, the mo chance I got of gettin' AIDS, so she can fo'get that shit.

I believe in supporting the gov'ment in they duty to he'p my kids so I was glad to see that I can pass my AIDS on t' dem. Wit' 15 kids, dough, it ain't no chance of much being lef. But if there is somethin' lef', can I pass my AIDS on to my momma?

The way I reads this stuff on AIDS, I see I can also get AIDS from blood transfusions and dirty heroin needles. So I am going to be signing up immediately for some transfusions at the hospital. Will the AIDS I get from dat be deducted from the AIDS I get from you? Do the dudes who give me the heroin needles have to give me the AIDS direct, or does I get that from your office? Oh, yea, I don't really know dat many peoples wit needles but heck of my pahtnas got pipes. So I tell you what —, I'ma collect some a dem and turn em in wit the needles so you could slip me a bonus.

Im a believer in getting all the AIDS I can, and I know dat my past record with yall prove dat. By the way, do I get my AIDS in monthly payments or every week? If I violate my parole again and have to go back to jail can I still get AIDS? Don't tell Shaniqua dis, but I still be havin sex in there, but its a whole different kind of thang, if you catch my meanin.

Hey that's a good Idea come to think of it, Can you get AIDS from sex wit men, 'cause even if I don't go back to da pen no time soon, Little JuJu, done wrote me a letter telling me he getting out Saturday at noon. He been on lock down fa a while an won't me to hep him out fa old time sake.

Yo paper say, Don't Die of Ignorance. You bet yo ass I ain't going to die without AIDS. I know my rights!

Your program supporter,

JOCKEY G

But, You Want a White Girl ...

BY *Ghetto Girl Blue*

The next time you are with her,
walking down the street,
don't act like you don't see me.
Cuz I'll be looking straight through you,
thinking...
I wish I could, lick you back into black existence
like a well-trained lioness,
I would,
Patrol the perimeters of your life
for our sworn enemies
slay them with a love that preexisted slavery
all so you would be fit and protected
for the journey that is your birthright
Every night I would, shamelessly
embrace your manhood
by the slick walls of my flippant mouth.
Let there forever be no doubt
my purpose here in the foreign land
is to lead you to the promise.
And like Harriet,
I would arm you
with the confidence of my faith,

Spread this soldier's thighs,
crown your head with my cave of salvation
And ride you into the shaft of time.
Can't you feel yourself,
even now,
as She lay beside you?
Pretty,
educated,
white privilege
So clean
that even her scent is tasteless.
But I am too dense
with victories and memories to
smell of anything but
hard work.
For I would if I could,
work out a sweat,
while we work out
the aggressions of this world,
until it too,
seeks the promised land deep inside
the black whole of my queendom.
And should you get weary
while on this journey,
I would run a bath of tenderness,
season it with fantasy
and whisk you away
... to a time when making love
wasn't making welfare babies
but the structuring of our story.
With every ounce of my river
I would quench your thirst for
woman I am
not the woman
Babylon has made me.

I would fame you "King,"
scream your name on command,
sit and spin on you man!
Even cum in your hand,
But damn...
You want a white girl.

Can I Please Have a Little More Cream?

BY *MT Promises*

I see you rollin' your eyes as you pass
switching your attitude along with you voluptuous ass
but don't be angry that I find your intensity too extreme
Oh, and can I please have a little more cream.

I've gained a little status from the things that I've learned
and I deserve a woman who is worth what I earn
I'm only trying to live the American dream
So, can I please, can I please have a little more cream.

You who can't seem to understand what I need
cutting me with that dual-bladed tongue 'till I bleed
You treat my success like part of some fast-money scheme
and you wonder why I ask for a little more cream.

It wasn't enough for me to spend eight years in college
and yet you still behave as if you have more knowledge.
You expect me to sit by passive as you holler and scream
so I've learned to appreciate the calmness of cream.

I'm not disregarding your strength or your beauty
but you treat me like supporting me as your king is not your duty
So chocolate, café au lait, mocha, latte, as sweet as you seem
Hold all the coffee, and can I please have a little more cream.

The Eunuch & Missy Frier

BY *Jessica Holter*

The Eunuch it seems
possessed magical charms
Though held in captivity,
bound by laws of slavery,
he roamed through cotton fields
as free as a slave's dream
of being free

His walk, more like a dance
held slave girls in trance
with his doe-like stride,
his legs stretched toes to hips
a great distance
His arms,
reaching nearly to their knees
His head held high in confidence
never given cause for penance
his nose always finding
and seizing a heavenly breeze
As graceful as the deer
finding rhythm in the air
as if the Frier plantation
had some freshness there

His hair was long
as soft as fur
His voice
as gentle as his manner
Never easy to stir
he could make the lion purr
with his manly strength
and is mothering nature

Born to Master Frier's father
Many years many years before the war
He was but a babe
when his mammy made
a solemn oath to God
that he would be her only child
born into subjugation
While weeding in the trash gang
a midwife from an island afar
told of berry and root
that could clean a pregnant womb

Tall and lean she stood
and when she sat she was
as the praying mantis
casting spells with
but the rub of her fingertips
A Caribbean witch,
is what they called her
Her name was Satajay
She took the new mother
into her council
and upon hearing her wishes
and considering her strife
she took mother and boy
to the end of her knife
taking kin and manhood away

The boy grew into something
less than a woman
but something much more than a man
Sensitivities and obedience
with strength in tongue and hand

Now war was coming, sure to ruin
the delicate balance of the South
And so it came to pass,
Master Frier was called to arms
but feared to leave his house
Wife and daughters
with chastity unguarded
to the whim of a manly bucks charms
and thusly he summoned
The Eunuch to his quarters

Take charge in my absence
ordered the Master
Guard with your life
my home, my children and my wife
and upon my return freedom shall be yours
So with his house in order
and his slaves in tact as cattle
Master Frier made a course
with his gun and his horse
to meet his fate in battle

Only days had passed
when at first Missy Frier asked
The Eunuch for his service
Upon finding no staff,
she lay on her back and gave herself as
she would be subject to a woman
without politic or grace
spilling upon his face
she came... so as never to return,
caring nothing of time or of fortune

So in the dark of night
and in the light of day
The Frier Plantation
and the hands that created it
slave, cattle, cotton and crop,
all slipped slowly away

The moral of this story is for
the man who measures worth
from where his length his hung,
For the definition of a lover
is not founded in the trouser
but in the sweetness of the tongue

At the dawn of the Civil War
three million black hands or more
tilled the Southern soil,
but The Eunuchs were far too gentle
even for cotton
Tis the tale of
The Eunuch and Missy Frier
Never to be forgotten

A Eunuch

A eunuch is a **castrated** human male—that is, a man who has had his testicles removed. The term "eunuch" can also refer to a man whose **penis** and **testicles** have been removed, or even to one who has had only his penis cut off. Young boys and **male infants** have been castrated in many societies for various reasons including to become **household protectors** posing no threat to women, for the **sexual servitude** of homosexual slave owners and in many European **churches** to sing in the choir! — www.rotten.com

Bed Bug

BY *Credence Malone*

I hopped a train
with a new white suit on my back,
a bed bug on my shoulder
Should I...
Should I
Kill it?
Bound for North

The music changed
while I was on the train,
cuz somebody choked Bessie
and Billie couldn't save her
cuz she was waiting for the blues man
backstage.

I saw the pale hand reach out to me
"I just want to get the bug off..."

North was a fat lazy bitch,
who thought somebody owed her something.

She sang too loud and her song was empty,
but she looked me in my face
with unearned pride
Her cold starry eyes weren't quite blue yet.
I watched her fat flabby arms ripple
like stripes on a phallic pole
She cloaked the freedom cape,
Danced the Watusi with jubilee
and named her kids from an
African name book

North was a greedy bitch.
She swallowed blues,
spit out Jazz
and called it Soul

"Put it back,
put it back!"
I told the white hand.
"White folks
can't stand
to see us
have nothin!"

Put the fucking
bed bug
back
on my shoulder!"

It was
a slow ride
back south.

I welcomed the heat.
Master was gone
cuz he,
couldn't afford
not afford us no more.

But I stayed on
that nameless
plantation
with a whispering willow
dripping a
unsung hero's blood
into a pool
that shown Bessie face.

Took root in an old shack,
and sometimes
basked in the scent
of my old Master
on my pillow,
till I was old,
ugly
and
ornery

daily daring North
to try to take
my South
from me again.

Sex After Trauma

Sexual abuse survivors often have trauma issues that impact their relationships, sexuality and ways of relating sexually. Survivors may develop Post Traumatic Stress Disorder, depression, sexual addiction or sexual avoidance, chemical dependency and alcoholism, dissociative disorders, borderline personality disorder, social discomfort and fear of people, and frequently have problems dealing with their anger.

Putting the pieces of your life back together after sexual trauma can be difficult. The first step in recovery is recognizing yourself, not as a "Sexual abuse Victim," but as a "SURVIVOR"!

Natural Healing
for Unnatural Pain
BY *The Head Doctor*

It is time, my sisters, to leave our burdens at the altar. We must learn to love to embrace and to respect our Punany without living in frustration with and compromising for the fear of others.

Your body is the reason the world still believes in magic. Have you seen what that thing can do?

Your Punany is the source of your greatest natural pain and the catalyst of your greatest pleasure
...in fact, your clitoris is the only sexual organ in the human body—male or female, whose only purpose is to give you pleasure.

Some may support this spell of mother nature
calling it a necessary gift

Still others argue to remove this
little pressure cooker immediately

Man fears what he does not understand
Is your Punany understood?

Is she a bargaining tool, to negotiate your lifestyle
or just a conciliation prize of womanhood?

Is she the ultimate force of human nature,
or just the consumer's measure of your worth?

Is she a weakness or a virtue?
or the price for which your affections are bought and sold

Is your Punany a blessing or do you treat her like a curse?

Are your memories of her something wonderful to behold?

Answer your own questions and you will find natural healing in truth.

Fucking

BY *Ghetto Girl Blue*

Ask me who I am.
I am a writer.
Poor, unreasonably logical
Jealous,
Obscene as the streets
that raised my generation,
Babies of the original X
Ruthlessly hunting for
a new chapter,
a deeper depth,
a higher height
Closure.
Creating drama in my wake
fantasy in my stead
Because I can't sleep at night with
ghetto gospel gasping for life,
beating the ministry
of raw dog truth in my head.

Ask me who I am.
I am a fucking woman.
No, not like that,
say it like this
I am the kind of woman
who loves to fuck
and to be fucked,
Tormented intellectually
between the fear that
this desire is a taboo
created by my rapist,
my molester
and the imagining that
sensuality is good,
and that it is
OK to exercise too
because I am a woman
through and through

Ask me who I am.
I am Punany.
The resurrection of the pussy
and the death of female castration.
No matter the political persuasion
they love to hear me say
"I love to be fucked."
They come in crowds of cheer
Donning the revolution like scarlet rags
Making families of women who love to be bad
Some listen quietly, mentally masturbating
in bible-studded conservative corners
and arm themselves with two-edge tongues
advancing to cut off my clit.
But I have erected a new understanding
That my clit is my dick
and I am too hard to surrender to religious bullshit

They should know after Panthers,
and rappers opened first eyes
One can not silence the urban wit

Ask me who I am.
I am a political prisoner of my art.
Draining the ink of my pen on your heart,
Coming harder.
So Let them enslave some
"third eye, head dressed, take another herbal remedy,
to naturally tame the beast in me, motherfuckers"
Make them to build a golden cross
and crucify the bitch in me
But I shall become a martyr
and come again, even harder.

Ask me who I am.
I am sick and tired of being sick and tired.
Give me a shrink
some sedatives, a house, a car
a man to blaze my fire,
drive me crazy, pay the rent, wash my car
he doesn't have to be loyal, just be present.
And, while you're at it,
get me some Barbie-like,
Silicone-inflated,
images
of what I am supposed to be
and drill them in my prepubescent mind
So I can find my way to social acceptance.
Yea, give me a good brainwashing and a make-over and you
could convince me of just about anything
Anything that is, accept putting down my pen
Cause a material woman's got to have a home
and this is where I live
The lines of this rhyme art my daily bread.

Ask me who I am.
I am a writer who hated being a fucking kid.
No, not like that,
say it like this,
I hated being the pretty, long-haired,
light-skinned, stuck-up
Passive-aggressive kid
that grown men wanted to fuck
You know the one?
She will inevitably become her mother's own enemy?
But even back then,
getting pushed into the popcorn stand,
jumped and caressed by girls in the bathroom,
I loved the fucking stage
Drama just wasn't a drama without the crowd
Give me a pen, a pad, a stage, some lights
and Barbie didn't stand a fucking chance
This stage is where I took my blackness back
and made it my center
Black art is the duality of reality and fiction
Like ghetto-born winners before me
I will live my art and teach while I do it
In the way that I do best
taming the beasts with the sensuality in me
mind fucking if I want to
not because they allow me.

Don't trip, see
I could be fucking with your families
Seducing men and women who don't belong to me
Or I could be a club ho, fucking just to fuck
I mean actually working a "real job"
So I can fuck for fucking free.
I could just say fuck it
and let the real ho in me free

I could get a pimp with a Porsche
and work like a horse
and bury this sexual revolution on the track
I bet they would fucking love that!

Ask me who I am.
I am a fucking woman, who hated being a fucking kid
A prisoner of my art, sick and tired of being sick and tired
and a minister if the raw dog truth
I am a writer,
Unfolding Ghetto Cinderella on command of my pen
So that fucking
won't fucking kill me.

Now, Ask me who I am again?

Old School Rules

BY *Jessica Holter*

"Get that bum out of my house!"

Momma just had a way of talking
that hurt sometimes but she was usually right
so what could an
Urban Maiden do?

Not much to choose from in the hood,
no telling who a girl might bring through
But Momma was more than a woman
she was a Momma,
hired by the government
to set our potentially wayward
foster child asses straight.

I hated her then, and love her so much today

I wish things hadn't gone so bad
that she would have to erase our lives
from her mind in her old age
all she can say now is that I was her "nice girl"

But back then I was her "gifted fool"
with an affinity for loving things
that she always felt were beneath me.

Of sex
(a subject she didn't enjoy the discussion of)
she's kept it very plain
"After your first time
you'll be using douche
for the rest of your life."

He invited me to a movie
came to pick me up in a van.
This boy
Blue-black
keen nose and well-defined full lips
So fine
(by my Blaxploitation flick induced definition)

"I reckon
you done
lost yo
cotton
picking
mind!"
She exclaimed.
Loud.
Very Loud
In front of the house
for any interested neighboring boy to hear
Then she got Bible on his ass...

"My girl ain't going nowhere in that lions den!"

I was flushed with embarrassment
walking, shamefully, back into the house
I didn't know if I was embarrassed because she
clowned me...
(that's what we called it back then)
...or if that was the moment I first realized

I Had No Game.

Notwithstanding,
I returned every piece of jewelry
any boy ever gave me

"Ain't nothin' for free.
Men's don't give you nothing,
less'n they want somethin'" in return.

Whatchu ready to give' em, girl?"

What do I do with the money Daddy gives me to wash his hair
and pluck the hairs from his face?
I was only thinking it, but she could read minds,
snatching thought from your head like a gypsy

"Nobody likes a Flippant woman."

How could I defend my teenaged longings for intimacy
against a woman with
The Sight?

The fear of her power overwhelmed me.

I saw her see something one day

glass break.

Then Auntie called the camp grounds
where we got away from Oakland attitudes
from time to time,
because Daddy knew that was important
and because Momma knew, if she didn't go
Daddy would have a license to commit a sin of omission
(The kind that fake saints think ain't a sin
if don't nobody know but God.)

"Sho Nuff,
Just like I seen it, the glass in the window
above my head board was broke," she told a friend.

We had committed a sin,
leaving the house unattended...
and a new foster daughter
with a bad brother in her family had just moved in.

"They even stole the Bible," she said sadly.

(The big white one will the hologram of the Lord's Supper on it.
You know the one.)

The big white book was in a house up the street
with coffee stains on it
because new aged slaves
didn't know a thing about old school game
Rules that kept you humble and on point
because you knew
that there was always something or someone
bigger, sharper, faster, and more witty than you.

(Men of my Momma's time didn't spend a lifetime in jail.
They served a spell and lived to tell.)

Ever have GAME stare you in the face
and you look right back at it, clueless?

I was too busy thinking how I'm gone get my daddy
off of me without telling her that I had ever let it happen
(In Old School Rules, it is the female who controls these
physical things.)

I secretly hoped she was just an old fogey
who could only guess about real life...
But deep inside I knew she could be as true as the Bible
and all sins against Biblical wisdom
were punishable by Hell's fire.

So I listened and obeyed
mostly out of fear

Her tongue was like
a switch from the old plum tree
she used for making preserves.

"Spare the rod spoil the child."

"If a man ain't got somebody,
he must not be worth havin'."

"This is going to hurt me... more..."
(Go on finish it...)

"A little bird told me."
(That's the one I hated most,
because I thought I was smarter
than everybody else.)

So what,
I snuck to my boyfriend's school.
A straight "A" student
and the teachers were on strike

I took two buses
on the promise of making out
with a boy that went to my church
and...
son of my momma's best friend

"A Gifted Fool"

That morning my sister had told Momma she was going to
school early to take the "gifted test"

Not for going but for allowing my disobedience and stupidity
to be witnessed and reported...

She plain
beat my ass,
Old School

Stunted Growth

BY *D.J. Blackmon*

I shaved my pussy, now the hair won't grow
'cause cut down thangs, don't come back in the ghetto.

I tried all I could, to encourage it to grow,
But nothing mattered, it ain't coming back no mo'

I watch a man cut down a tree,
While constantly staring down at me,
His smug looks don't really matter, see?
Cause I'm the one who controls what I be.

I watch my pussy, to see if there's any hair there now,
I have a hope that I might get it to want to grow somehow.
But growth is hard when folks keep cutting you down.
How a king be respected, when you take away his crown?

The tree, its branches, its leaves, all laying on the ground
Its majesty and ancestry are no longer to be found.
I keep hoping since them shackles got loose,
that our minds would be unbound,
But it seems to me, the things I knew,
that used to be,
are no longer around.

See, growth takes courage, faith, work, belief and energy
We be like the weeds, wild,
but without growth, we be just like that tree.

There ain't no magic, no miracle grow,
and there ain't no simple balm,
Without growth, we just be children
with no pussy hair,
and upturned hands
with no solution in the palm.

Daddy's Little Girl

BY *Ghetto Girl Blue*

They say to thine own self be true
But who are you?
Who were you then?
Who are you now?
Do you know?

Are you walking the path that Jesus lived?
Can you forgive your father when he has sinned?

How long will you forget and forgive
so that others may live?

Don't try to compromise my revolution
Ain't giving you no restitution
Though you're seeking soul solution
My love has long been dead

Every time I think of Daddy
Pain just well-up in my head
Can you change my constitution
From your death bed?

Daddy, daddy
What are you looking for?
Daddy, daddy
I don't want your money
I don't want to be your whore
OOO daddy, OOO daddy
I always had what you need
I know just what it feels like, when you bleed

When I was a little girl
you cheated my virginity
Now you're on your bed of death
you say, "Pray for me... Pray for me!"
What shall I do?
"Pray for you? Pray for you?"
oh no, see...
I'm a lying little Jezebel,
looking for a pass to hell
dirty little secrets to tell
Who will pray for me?

You ate my soul like cancer, Daddy
My blood is in that bed with you
and I'm still searching for the answer
To my blues

Don't try to compromise my revolution
Ain't giving you no restitution
Though you're seeking soul solution
My love has long been dead

Every time I think of Daddy
Pain just well-up in my head
Can you change my constitution
From your death bed?
Daddy, daddy
What are you looking for?
Daddy, daddy
I don't want your money
I don't want to be your whore
OOO daddy, OOO daddy
I always had what you need
I know just what it feels like, when you bleed

Pray for you, pray for you, What can I do?
Pray for you? Pray for you, Who'll pray for me?
Just what am I supposed to tell Jesus
I know you couldn't possibly mean this
Look into my eyes and see this
time it ain't gon' go your way

They say to thine own self be true
But who are you?
Who were you then?
Who are you now?
Do you know?
Are you walking the path that Jesus lived?
Can you forgive your father when he has sinned?

About the Author

Also known as Ghetto Girl Blue, Jessica Holter is founder of The Punany Poets, a world-renowned poetic troupe who made history with a controversial erotic poetry and dance feature on HBO's *Real Sex* documentary series in the year 2000. Holter has also appeared on Black Entertainment Television, Playboy TV, Cinemax, London's channel 5 and the Independent Film Channel.

Holter has invited thousands of people all over the country to share in The Punany Experience in a live, interactive stage show.

She has self-published several titles including *Punany: The Hip Hop Psalms*, (Volumes I, II & III), *Speak the Unspeakable*, *AKA Dead Man*, *The Head Doctor's Sex Tales*, and *Verbal Penetration Volume I* before being discovered by bestselling author/publisher Zane who invited her into the Strebor Family in 2006.

Visit the author at www.jessicaholter.com or email her at ghettogirlblue@yahoo.com.

Author's Note

As an activist I am most dedicated to AIDS awareness because I feel it represents a larger problem among African American women. HIV/AIDS is the physical manifestation of our lack of self-love and self-esteem. I say to you "set boundaries, respect your self, increase your standards."

I was a "love child." The best thing my mother ever did for me was convince me of this idea.

As the story goes, the "free love" movement was narrowing to an end when my parents, a Jamaican man called Tarzan and an Irish woman named Jane Therese moved to Morning Star Ranch, a commune / nudist colony in Sebastopol, California where they lived in a tent for a few years with my brothers. But by the time I was born in 1969, my brothers were in juvenile hall, my mother was certified "insane," and my father was in jail.

But I was a "love child." So even as I was shuffled through the foster care system, I believed that I was loved. My confidence in aspiring to excel beyond what anyone would have ever expected of a girl of my pedigree is based in the fact that I am loved.

I never met my father, Jessie Donovan Simpson, but I am told that I am but one of 22 children that he fathered by the time he was 39. I am looking forward to finding my family someday soon.

My greatest blessing was not becoming a writer, a performer, an activist or a publisher. My greatest blessing was in becoming a mother. I thank God for allowing me to become part of the family of women who have known the pain, the sacrifice and the glory of giving life.

**Look for more from the Punany Poets
2008**

If you're interested in more of the Punany experience, visit
www.verbalpenetrationbook.com